# THE HOUSEWIFE ASSASSIN'S DEEP STATE DEEP FAKE BAKE-OFF

The Housewife Assassin Series
Book 25

JOSIE BROWN

## Praise for Josie Brown's Novels

"The last book that made me laugh: *The Housewife Assassin's Handbook*. Brown's unorthodox surprises did make me laugh. I taught it in a class about comic novels."
Jane Smiley, Pulitzer Prize-Winning Author

"This book hits all the right notes...I now want a week at the beach to read them all...I'm completely smitten."
Barbara Vey

"On many days, I'll join deep discussions about the works of Le Carré, Deighton, Greene, Ambler, and Forsyth. And then I take incredible delight in a series like *The Housewife Assassin*. Just the name would likely cause eyebrows to be raised, and likely, my stature as an 'expert' falls a bit. Too bad! I read for enjoyment. The authors mentioned above all entertained the heck out of me. And so does Josie Brown's wonderfully fun and amusing series about Donna Stone."
Randall Masteller, *Spy Guys + Gals*

"Brown writes the kind of feminist action plot that men should be reading, especially male authors, to cure that trope of 'vapid sexy girl with a gun.' There's enough comedy sprinkled in between the emotional scenes and within the action to keep readers' minds from going too grim here. As for the sex scenes, these are the best I've ever read. No airy poetry and metaphors. Brown accomplishes setting the mood whether Donna is willing and able or whenever Donna isn't sure what she wants. Brown's hired gun plot is fun, sometimes aggravating, and filled with the wonderful twist of being from a mother's POV."

Amber Love

# Novels in The Housewife Assassin Series

*The Housewife Assassin's Tips for*
*Weddings, Weapons, and Warfare*
(Book 11)

*The Housewife Assassin's Husband Hunting Hints*
(Book 12)

*The Housewife Assassin's Ghost Protocol*
(Book 13)

*The Housewife Assassin's Terrorist TV Guide*
(Book 14)

*The Housewife Assassin's Deadly Dossier*
(Book 15: The Series Prequel)

*The Housewife Assassin's Greatest Hits*
(Book 16)

*The Housewife Assassin's Fourth Estate Sale*
(Book 17)

*The Housewife Assassin's Horrorscope*
(Book 18)

*The Housewife Assassin's White House Keeping Seal of Approval*
(Book 19)

*The Housewife Assassin's Assassination Vacation Planner*
(Book 20)

*The Housewife Assassin's Antisocial Media Tips*
(Book 21)

*The Housewife Assassin's Manners, Missiles, and Mayhem*

(Book 22)

*The Housewife Assassin's Gambit*

(Book 23)

*The Housewife Assassin's Underwater Assets*

(Book 24)

*The Housewife Assassin's Deep State Deep Fake Bake-Off*

(Book 25)

# Dieting Before Thanksgiving

*Is it worth it? Do the math:*

*Let's say you'll put on five pounds over the Thanksgiving weekend. (In truth, you put on seven, but why tell the world?)*

*A typical Thanksgiving feast has turkey, dressing, and gravy (350 calories); some mashed potato (sweet, at 249 calories—or Idaho with gravy 280 calories); cranberry sauce (quarter-cup: 100 calories); some green dish made more palatable with something that makes you forget it's green (say green bean-mushroom soup casserole with 360 calories), at least a glass of wine (120 calories), and at least one piece of pie (350 calories) ...*

*Oh, who do you think you're kidding? Of course, you're going to eat more than one piece—*

*—and of different pies, at that!*

*All this before your crazy uncle annoys you, and you take a second or third glass of wine...*

*Now you've got around 3,000-plus calories in you!*
*That's a heck of a lot to walk off—*
*Before the next day, when you chow down on leftovers.*
*Solution: fast for the rest of the weekend.*
*Now you know where the term "cold turkey" originated.*

---

THE PARTY at the German consulate in Los Angeles is a sparkling affair. Though Deutschland's Thanksgiving takes place in October, it has postponed its holiday to the Sunday before America's national feasting day for diplomatic reasons. Instead of Thanksgiving turkey, fixings, and pies—its buffet version is a cornucopia of Germany's traditional dishes. There is a succulent sauerbraten, potato pancakes, pan-roasted carrots, and speckbohnen, a German green bean dish with bacon.

Because I haven't eaten all day—make that all week, knowing I'd have to squeeze into this form-hugging mini—I'm voracious and eyeing the dishes like a kid salivating in Willy Wonka's Chocolate factory. Unable to resist any longer, I reach for a potato pancake when my date, Barry Telford, an Austin, Texas-based tech engineer who works for a pop-up VPN, pats my bottom—something he does using any excuse and all too often—and wags his finger at me. "Now, now, *Liebling*, none of that," he chides. "Your curves have enough, er, gusto."

*Grrrrr! Son of a bitch! As if!* And saying so in his West

Texas accent and with a German endearment doesn't make it any better.

Instead, I giggle as if his teasing was precious. In truth, I'm curbing the urge to stick my fork in his eye for being impertinent. Maybe I'd feel differently if he wasn't just built for comfort but sits down in shifts, too.

Whereas Barry hired me to attend as his arm charm, his real reason for being here has nothing to do with the holiday, the food, or the company and everything to do with what he'll soon give and receive via a brush-pass with another guest, soon to be determined. For a Bitcoin soft wallet containing a billion-dollar payday, Barry will hand off an SD card containing a software trojan that his buyer wishes to embed somewhere that I haven't been told. Apparently, it's above my pay grade.

So be it. I do know that, should Barry's contact succeed, a terrorist act will be initiated. Unfortunately, the who, what, and when—not to mention how—is yet to be determined until Acme can decipher this intel.

We'll get it out of Barry in the worst possible way.

At least he's enjoying a hell of a last meal.

The cell conversation in which Barry and his contact discussed the brush pass happened yesterday, here in the consulate. It was intercepted by a diplomatic intelligence officer stationed here for Germany's intelligence service, *der Bundesnachrichtendienst,* or BND for short. However, the day the call was intercepted was a hectic and full house. It could have been made by anyone traveling through the consulate at that moment: tourists or Americans applying for visas and citizenship. So that nothing could go wrong for one of Germany's allies on its territory (an embassy or consulate is considered native soil to the country that built it), Germany hired my black ops organization, Acme Industries, to intercept the transaction. Since Acme's fee will be the Bitcoin wallet's funds, it took the assignment. *Cha-ching! Early Christmas bonuses for everyone!*

Yesterday, the contracted party organizers were also on hand. But they, the caterers, and the cleaning staff have been used by the consulate for at least a decade and have already been vetted.

Though Barry has never met his contact, he'll know the person when he hears this password: "Try the pie. It's out of this world."

Barry is to respond: "Wish I could, but I'm watching my weight."

Considering he's quite a heifer, that's believable. It would be even more so if he hadn't already snarfed down so much schnitzel. But, hey, Barry is a nervous eater, especially when a billion dollars is on the line. Once Barry says the abracadabra phrase, his cell will buzz with confirmation of payment to his soft wallet.

The contact will then answer. "Ah, come on, live a little."

Barry will acquiesce. At the same time, he'll then pass the SD card by shaking the contact's hand.

Arnie Locklear, my team's tech op, is my date's limo driver. While waiting for our departure, which will happen immediately after the brush pass, he's already hacked into the consulate's security feeds and all CCTV within a six-block radius.

Emma Honeycutt—Arnie's wife and our ComInt director—monitors our actions through Arnie's SecCam handiwork. The whole team wears earbuds for audio and contact lenses with a video feed.

One intriguing clue: the caterer claims that one of the consulate's staff specifically requested that Oom-Pah-Pah Bakery make the bite-sized mini-pies to be passed forward to the hundred guests. The man gave a phone number, though the caterer can't recall the man's name.

Oom-Pah-Pah Bakery doesn't exist. Its phone number, which was live when the order was placed, is now disconnected. And yet, the caterer received the pies this morning, as promised.

Per Acme's instructions, the consulate clarified to the caterer that only three people would be circulating with the mini pies. They comprise the rest of my mission team: Dominic Fleming, Abu Nagashahi, and my husband and co-team leader, Jack Craig. They're wearing tuxedos. Granted, our British honey trap, Dominic's, is bespoke: from Saville Row. In other words, he's better dressed than some of the guests.

Jack and Abu brought metal detectors to run over the pies, but when they saw the pie pans were aluminum, they realized looking for an SD card or thumb drive in one of them would be like looking for a needle in a haystack.

Now that my three team members are roaming through the crowd with the dessert trays, Barry's contact will soon be upon us. Knowing this, Abu hovers at his elbow.

Suddenly, Barry and I hear these words: "Try the pie. It's out of this world."

Barry responds as directed: "Wish I could, but I'm watching my weight."

The contact then gives the agreed-upon passcode: "Come on, live a little." He proffers the pie to Barry.

Abu's eyes dart to the stranger. He frowns as if he recognizes him. But the way he shakes his head, he can't seem to place him.

"Gee...he looks familiar," Emma Honeycutt admits too.

She's right—sort of. The man is tall and broad-shouldered. His hair is auburn, as is his mustache. But his face has creases, so he's either wearing fake hair, or it's a dye job. Another telltale sign is that he stoops slightly, which makes me guess he's over seventy. It's too bad he wears tinted glasses because I can't see the color of his eyes.

Still, I wonder: *How do I know this guy?*

Jack is close enough that the man can take one of the pies from his tray. He hands it to Barry—

Jack looks at the suspect just as the men shake hands. His double-take indicates he, too, feels he knows the contact somehow.

"The intel was in Barry's brush pass," Emma declares.

"Not to worry. We're on him," Jack mutters.

Aw, heck—

*Barry ate the pie!*

Gah! Now, I'll have to go home with him, force-feed him

a laxative, and wait for the thumb drive to come out the other end.

In other words, dominatrix cosplay. Granted, Barry will be into it. Me? *Not so much.*

I lace my arm through Barry's. "Can we get out of here now?"

"Sure, babycakes! Let's go back to the hotel and celebrate." He practically pulls me to the consulate's front door.

At the same time, Jack, Abu, and Dominic are ducking and dodging through the milling crowd. They want to apprehend Barry's contact and retrieve the precious intel.

By the time Barry and I return to the limo, he's huffing and puffing. Worse yet, he's pale as a ghost. I slip in first when Arnie exits the front seat to open the door for us. But Arnie needs to help Barry through the door—

Who then collapses onto me.

Arnie jumps back into the front seat, starts the car, and drives off. But since I'm pinned under Barry and the privacy panel is up, Arnie doesn't know that I'm struggling to breathe—

Which is more than Barry is doing right now. He's got no pulse, and he's just wet himself—and me too.

I wonder why Emma doesn't see my predicament. When I focus on the video feed coming in on my lenses, I see why:

Jack has cornered Barry's contact in an alley. He's drawn his gun to shoot him, but then Jack freezes. Instead, he walks up to him and snatches off the red wig.

The man is about to turn around—

But then the man's face whites out when a car's head-lights hit it full-on—

And suddenly, Jack's video feed blacks out.

---

EMMA SHOUTS, "Man down—*and it's Jack*! Arnie, turn the limo around. He's in the alley behind the consulate! Abu and Dominic, the suspect is getting away...make that *two of them*! Get there as fast as you can!"

As the limo does a U-Turn, Barry's body rolls off me.

Abu and Dominic are already there when Arnie makes it to the alley. Jack is rubbing the back of his head to ease the pain of what hit him.

"What happened?" I ask.

"I...saw...*a ghost,*" he mutters.

"What do you mean?"

"Someone who...was supposedly dead. It was long before you and I knew each other." Jack shakes his head. "Where is Barry?"

"In the limo," I reply. "But... Unfortunately, he's dead, too. When we get back to Acme, the first thing Ryan will want to do is have him autopsied."

Jack guffaws. "I'm not surprised. In the case of my ghost, it's par for the course."

"What do you mean?"

"It's his M.O. He suckers someone to do his bidding with the promise of a big payday, only to get nothing. Or, in this case, worse: to end up dead." Jack shrugs. "My guess?

We'll discover that Barry has been poisoned and that whatever he ate won't lead to a fat payday."

*Shite.* "Don't leave me in suspense. Who's your ghost?"

"I...I can't answer that."

"Can't? Or won't?"

"Donna, believe me, it's classified 'Top Secret.' Maybe you'll get Ryan to wrangle clearance for you."

*As if.*

Tenderly, I touch the bloody spot on Jack's head. "You were hit pretty hard."

"That doesn't surprise me, either. My ghost's accomplice has always had it out for me."

"I assume you know that person, too—"

Whoever came to rescue Jack's assailant.

Jack frowns but says nothing.

"Bloody hell! It's as if the targets have disappeared into thin air!" Dominic's growl interrupts us.

Emma shifts our video feeds to Dominic's sight line. He's right. He's standing in an alley with no exits or fire escapes.

"Same here. The egress dead-ends on a wall against the highway," Abu replies.

"Emma, what can you see via an aerial scan?" I ask.

A moment later, she admits, "No one on foot. I'll scan the last five minutes of the SatCom feed to see any pedestrians moving into parked vehicles and driving off. Honestly, there's so much traffic that even ten minutes of reconnaissance may take a while, especially since we don't know exactly who we're looking for."

"Jack recognized both culprits," I inform her. "But apparently, we don't have clearance for their dossiers."

"It's something Ryan will only want to discuss face-to-face with me." His step is shaky, so he takes the arm I offer. "We should head back to the office and get his wrath over so you can go home and bake your pies."

"Oh my God—I almost forgot that Thanksgiving is just three days away! I've got to get to the grocery store!"

"You'll be happy to know that Trisha and Jeff realized you were otherwise engaged and took it upon themselves to stock the kitchen with your traditional provisions for everyone's favorite food fest." Jack chuckles. "Or, as Jeff calls it, 'Mom's-Giving.'"

"You forgot the second half of that nickname, at least after Jeff finishes the meal: 'Mom's Giving Me the Tummy Ache of the Century,'" I remind him.

"And then there's Trisha's name for it: 'Mom's Giving Me an Extra Ten pounds.'" Jack counters.

I chuckle. "How many times do I have to tell our kids, 'Let moderation be your guide?'"

"Spoken like a true Roman philosopher." Jack rolls his eyes. "In either regard, this mission is aborted—and Ryan will be hunting our scalps." He pauses in thought. "Here's an idea. How about inviting him to Thanksgiving? That should soften him up."

"You're quite aware that I invite him every year, right? And every year, he passes. He makes up some excuse about spending it with some gang of poker playing spooks he keeps in contact with."

"That's the perfect reason to invite him: because he'll say he can't come. See? I've thought of everything." Jack taps the side of his head but then flinches from the pain.

"It's worth trying if only to hear him lower his voice to a decent decibel." I shrug. "Okay, let's do it."

"Donna and Jack, I assume you'll want me to delete this little side conversation?" Emma's question causes me to grimace.

*Yikes.*

"Um...yes, please." Jack's murmur couldn't be humbler.

"Then how about a little tit for tat?" Emma replies. "Like, say, allowing the Honeycutt-Locklear party of three to join you for Mom's Giving?"

Still, I must ask, "I thought you always trek out of state to Arnie's folks' place for Thanksgiving."

Emma guffaws. "Not this year, thank goodness! They're going on a cruise. They are finally fed up with his sister Eloise's insistence on cooking every dish and then burning them all. The piece de resistance was her husband's attempt last year to smoke the turkey. He threw it in the smoker, frozen! I'm sure it went high enough that NASA classified it as an Unidentified Aerial Phenomenon. And since I can't cook..." Emma's pause is her way of verifying that they won't be intruding.

Jack looks at me.

I nod.

"Sure," Jack and I say in unison, proof we'll do anything to keep to our strategy to lessen Ryan's tirade.

"*Wahoo!* I can't wait to tell Arnie!" Emma's shout is

worthy of a 'Bama football fan after a successful Hail Mary pass.

"Hold your news from him until we're back at Acme," I plead. I don't want to tell her that hearing Arnie is joining us will undoubtedly be the nail in the coffin for Ryan to pass on the honor. He's made no bones about his dismay over Arnie's table manners.

"Okay, mum's the word," she promises.

I help Jack to his feet, but when I offer my arm for him to lean on, he refuses it. He's bracing for delivering an even bigger disappointment to Ryan:

The intel we lost.

More so, the fee it would have earned Acme.

# 2

# Pre-Event Prep

*The best holiday meals begin with preparations made in advance. No need to get whipped up into a frenzy when realizing you're out of eggs before you've even made your last pie!*

***Rule #1: Shop early.*** *By getting there when the store opens, you'll avoid crowded aisles. You'll also run through them like the winning contestant in a shopping spree! (Considering how full your cart—or two—will be, you'll wish that were the case.)*

***Rule #2: Shop thoroughly.*** *Make a list. Before you go to the cash register line, check it twice. However, if you've missed something, bat your eyes seductively and ask the person in front of you to keep an eye on your cart while you race through the store to grab the missing item before the cashier is ready to ring you up. Sure, it would be great if your Good Samaritan was a Really Great Samaritan and paid for your* *provisions, too—but don't count on it. You'll be lucky if they're still hanging around when you return.*

*(You'll be luckier still if they didn't and if your cart hasn't been picked clean by those who thought it was abandoned.)*

***Rule #3: When in doubt, over-shop!*** *Afraid you won't have enough stuffing? Just to be sure, double your usual purchase. The same goes for potatoes and Karo syrup for your pecan pies—not to mention your frozen pie shells. Best case scenario: you'll treat yourself and your family to a second Thanksgiving when no one wants to visit—say, in February!*

---

AS EXPECTED, Ryan is pacing in the conference room. The second after Jack has closed its door, he roars, "What in hell happened out there?"

Even Arnie, who's usually oblivious to Ryan's moods, is left wide-eyed. Sinking into his seat, he exclaims, "I enlarged and slo-mo'ed the security footage. It seems that Barry's contact pressed something into the mini pie before handing it to him. We've got his corpse on a slab in Acme's morgue. The item, an SD card, was still in his stomach. It's being surgically removed as we speak."

"Since he was poisoned, I doubt seriously it'll contain anything, let alone the supposed Bitcoin account containing his fee," Ryan growls. "And it doesn't forgive the fact that Barry's contact that your team allowed the contact to walk away with the intel." His head pivots to Jack. "Mr. Craig, why the hell did you let him get away?"

Just now, my cell buzzed with a text from Mary:

**Mom, call me when you can. I've got something I'd like to discuss.**

*Lousy timing, sweet Mary.*

As if also preparing for Ryan's wrath, Jack, raises both hands as if bracing himself for a second cyclone of curses to follow this already-loaded question. "I was blindsided by... well, by an old nemesis." He glances around the table. "Someone whose file is above the security clearance grade of the rest of our team."

Ryan opens his mouth to speak but then closes it. A long two minutes later, he growls, "Everyone clears the room —*except for Jack.*"

He doesn't have to ask twice. The stampede to the door brings Abu and me shoulder to shoulder in the doorframe.

"Hey, what happened to 'ladies first?'" I hiss.

"I thought you were all about equal rights for all," he counters.

He's right—

Which is why I shove past him—

Only to be pushed aside by Dominic—

Who doubles over as I throw an elbow into his gut.

Righting himself, he whines, "Not very ladylike, madam!"

I hoot, "This, from a man who claims to be a gentleman! Well, sir, actions speak louder than words—"

Emma's whistle is loud enough to stop taxis several

blocks away. So, yep, it gets our attention: "Enough already, folks! Goodness, I haven't seen a crowd scrimmage like this since the last Bears-Packers game! If you keep it up, I won't be able to read Ryan's lips to see who the heck got away!"

Proof that Abu, Dominic, Arnie, and I get her excellent point is the casual poses we strike while following her lead. As for Abu, he's leaning back in his chair with his feet on his desk and looks up at the convex security mirror with a dead-on view of the conference room. Arnie's computer screen shows a video feed of what is in front of him: the conference room. As for me, I grab a compact from my purse. While pretending to re-apply my gloss, I angle it to read my boss's lips.

Why am I not surprised when I find Dominic also holding a mirror? A much bigger one, I might add. He pretends to comb his hair while aiming it at Ryan and Jack.

"Who is the guy Jack just mentioned?" Arnie asks. "Someone named 'Namdlo.' But that name doesn't sound Russian."

I mutter, "It's not, you ninny! In fact, it's not a name in any language. Just because you're looking in a mirror doesn't mean you must read what he says backward."

Arnie frowns, perplexed.

Abu groans. "That a boy! Go to the head of the class." He turns to Emma. "How can he claim to be a tech genius when he can't even figure that out?"

She wags her finger at him. "Not a genius. A *savant*. And not just any ol' savant, but one prefaced with the word 'idiot.'"

Abu nods sagely. "Ah! I stand corrected."

"Back on topic, folks. What do we know about this Namdlo guy?" I ask.

Emma turns back to her computer. As she taps away, she grumbles, "A dossier under that name isn't in our database.'"

Dominic harrumphs. "When has that ever stopped you before?"

She frowns because she knows he's got a point, then she gives me a sidelong glance:

In other words, she's leaving it up to me if she should go against Ryan's wishes and request it from the CIA.

I can't put her in that position.

Sighing, I murmur, "Don't chance it, Emma."

Abu guffaws. "Not when you can do the voodoo you do so well, Mrs. Craig. And if you get it out of him, release a smoke signal. Inquiring minds want to know."

I smile like a Sphynx, but I make no promises. Since our last mission, Jack and I have been in a delicate place. Neither of us wants to push the other too far, let alone away.

Asking too many questions is the worst way to do either.

Could I wheedle it out of him? Possibly. But would it be worth losing his trust?

The answer is no.

So, instead, I change the subject. "Before Jack passed out, he saw someone else. Was even a second of it picked up by his video feed?"

Emma nods. "Exactly half a second. I was just about to ask Ryan for clearance to trace it through the InterPol Visual

Analysis Database, but then he blew his stack. Maybe I should wait on that until he's done with Jack."

Speak of the devil! Jack walks out of Ryan's office.

Noting this, Emma shakes her head, signaling it's time to change the subject.

Following Emma's lead, I give her a bright smile and exclaim, "I can't wait to see which pie little Nicky likes the best."

"If he's like me, he'll eat them all," Arnie assures me.

Emma sighs rapturously. "My favorite is your cherry."

"I'll wager my hot toddy fruit cake bests it," Dominic boasts. "Or my Lincolnshire plum bread! That, and a good dry sherry, will give any pie a run for its money. And a *truly excellent* sherry is anything but cheap." He pauses. "As the proverbial Greek bearing such exquisite gifts, your invitation is accepted."

Jack does a double-take but keeps his mouth shut. Instead, he pulls his mobile from his pocket and starts texting.

The next thing I know, my cell buzzes. Nonchalantly, I glance down at my desk to read it.

## JACK

*WHAT THE HELL HAPPENED? DID DOMINIC JUST INVITE HIMSELF TO THANKSGIVING?*

## DONNA

*Seems to be the case! Like you, I cringe at the thought, but it would be rude not to let him come. If you remember, we spent a year living with Dominic when we had to blow up the house because the Feds raided us.*

## JACK

*How could I forget? He brings it up whenever he wants a favor. The quid pro quo never seems to end.*

I'VE JUST NOTICED that Abu has turned his chair away from us.

Jack has picked up on this, too. He taps Abu's shoulder. "Hey, if you're available, why not spend Thanksgiving with us?"

Abu is all smiles again. "That would be awesome!"

"Great! We'll have a full house then," I declare. I catch Jack's eyes, then nod toward Ryan's office.

Jack frowns, then shakes his head. He failed at his mission: appeasing Ryan with our invitation.

So that we're not the first of our team out the door, we spend a half-hour writing the recap of our mission's failure, then take off.

WE'RE on the road just ten minutes before Jack comes out with it: "As you can imagine, Ryan wasn't too happy about the mission."

"I figured as much." I pat his arm. "Well, maybe he'll change his mind about Thanksgiving."

"Doubtful. Believe me, I tried. He passed. The topic is closed."

"Is there anything I can do?"

"To console me?" He arches a brow. "Heck yeah! I'll meet you in the playhouse as soon as we can escape the kids."

"You know that wasn't what I meant," I chuckle. "But, yes, that too."

"After T-Day Prep, of course." Jack glances over.

"Not tonight, I'm too darn tired"—I bat my eyes—"for anything else but our rendezvous."

That puts a smile on Jack's face—

But then it disappears. "I hope you're not softening me up for a kiss-and-tell session."

*Darn it! Heck, yeah, I was...*

"If, by that, you mean I can't ask you what Ryan briefed you on, I thoroughly understand."

"I'm sorry, Donna. You know I would if I could—"

"It's...okay." But he knows it's not when I put my hand back in my lap.

"Message received," Jack grumbles. "Despite Ryan's absence, we'll have a pretty full house anyway, now that Dominic is also joining the party."

"He's got nowhere else to spend it. Jody is out of town on an assignment," I point out.

"Even during a major at-home holiday?" He snorts. "Where is she going this time?"

"A couple of TikTok influencers are tying the knot. She's coordinating the event. Dominic is beside himself. He thinks she's avoiding him."

"He may be right," Jack retorts. "Especially since he's never cut the cord with the other lady in his life."

I shrug. "Dominic is a fool. Teddy Twala toys with his affections like a cat who's caught a mouse between its paws."

The femme fatale is an MI6 operative who, on a recent mission, I'd mistaken for our suspect. It didn't help that she was also snuggling up to Jack because she suspected me for the same reason.

Yeah, I know. *Oops! My bad.*

"That's Dominic to a tee. He'd much rather moon over the impossible than appreciate the star within reach." Jack shrugs.

Suddenly, I realize how conveniently Jack changed the subject from the one that matters most: *who was the mystery man making the brush pass?*

When Ryan announces the mission is officially aborted, I'll get it out of Jack.

Which brings us to the one billion dollar question:

When *will* it be over?

Since the mission was a disaster, it may already be.

Fingers crossed that this is already the case.

Or at least until after Thanksgiving.

# 3

# Life of Pies

*When it comes to pies, fillings are the easy part. The crust can make or break your reputation as a baker. Here are a few never-fail tips:*

*First, get a good food processor. It makes mixing your crust ingredients (flour and salt first, then butter) a breeze.*

*Next, use the best high-fat European-style unsalted butter. (Suggestion: Plugra).*

*Also, use sea salt. Its larger grains add a flavor pop.*

*And finally, to enhance your fillings, consider adding a liquor. Make it one that compliments the flavor of the fruit or nut. Can't decide what to match with which pie? Experiment —but not too much. The last thing you need is to get tipsy and forget that your pies are in the oven.*

*However, if you do, scrape off the burnt part of your crust and turn your pie into a crumble.*

*It may not look as pretty, but the flavors are the same.*

MY HAPPY PLACE is my kitchen, especially as I make my Thanksgiving pies.

It's two o'clock on Monday morning. The rest of the household is now asleep. But when Jack and I got home from the office, all hands were on deck to prepare our side dishes to be served alongside the humongous uncooked turkey now cooling its meaty legs, juicy breasts, large wings, and plump thighs in the fridge. Jack peeled the Idaho spuds while Jeff mashed the yams and Trisha shelled peas. Since we've got to quadruple the provisions we'd purchased before the guest list grew, Jeff and Trisha were sent back to forage Hilldale Grocery's now emptied vegetable bins and shelves for whatever is left there. If the shelves are bare, they'd been given prior approval to pivot to suitable substitutes. For the next two days, we'll work in shifts to make enough to feed the army that will storm the picket gate fronting our faux Victorian on T-Day.

I've already rolled out the dough for eight pies: two each of apple, cherry, pumpkin, and pecan. The apple pies' top crust will be adorned with flour leaves, whereas the cherry pies will have a lattice crust. Each of my pies has a secret ingredient. For the pumpkin, it's Triple Sec. The pecan gets amaretto. I use a brandy with the apple and Campari with the cherry.

After putting the pies in the oven, I start the arduous process of cleaning up: putting leftover ingredients in the pantry and then stacking mixing bowls and utensils in the dishwasher. In time I see Jack's jacket hanging on one of the kitchen island's chairs. As I lift it to hang it up, a mobile phone drops out of one of its pockets.

It's not his personal one, but a burner.

*Odd.* Why would he have a second, untraceable phone?

As I suspected, it's locked with an extended alphanumeric code. It could be anything: his birthday or mine, or that of one of our kids. Our anniversary. The day we met.

It also uses fingerprint ID.

*Hmmm...*

Okay, yeah, I'm curious as to why he has it and where he got it. I guess I could wake him up and ask—

But no. He needs his sleep.

I could ask him when he wakes up later this morning—

But I'd hate to come off as a Nosy Parker...

Oh hell. Who do I think I'm kidding? Of course, I want to know—

Just like I know he'd do the same if he found a strange mobile in my pocket.

I check the kitchen for something he touched, but then I remember all the glasses are drying in the dishwasher.

Except for one: in our bathroom.

I grab a plastic bag. Then, silently, with the torch app on my phone, I make my way upstairs.

---

JACK'S BREATH IS STEADY. Still, I wait to see if he'll toss or turn in the next minute or two. He doesn't so I move to our bathroom when I'm sure he's sleeping deeply. Without turning on the light, I feel around his side of the sink for the glass he uses for mouthwash. I've just slipped it into the bag when an arm goes around my waist:

Jack's.

He nuzzles my neck and whispers, "Why aren't you in bed yet?"

When I turn to face him, my arm holding the glass goes behind my back. "The pies are still in the oven," I murmur. "The moment I pull them out to cool, I'll come back to bed —and to you. I promise."

"You always make this your Super Bowl," he chuckles. "Next Thanksgiving, let's leave the meal prep to some fancy restaurant."

"It's a lot of work, I know. But...well, I enjoy it." I sound like I mean it because I do.

I guess I'm a good liar because he leans into me and sighs. "It's one of the reasons I love you. Without you, I'm a nomad. Donna, you are my anchor."

Guilt surges through me. If he knew why I came up here, he'd be angry, and I'd be girl overboard on the Good Ship Jack Craig.

I don't deserve him.

I show my appreciation with a long, loving kiss. Holding me now as if he never wants to let me go only makes me feel worse.

I am betraying him.

Or am I saving him?

I won't know until I open that cell.

I'm doing it for Jack's own good.

At least, that's what I tell myself.

---

I WAIT five minutes to make sure Jack doesn't follow me downstairs. When I feel the coast is clear, I find a container of Play-Doh that the kids keep around for laughs. After flattening a piece into a disk, I press it against the glass.

Crossing my fingers, I put it on the cell's finger ID circle.

The cell opens.

I check the texts. There is only one. The name assigned: O.M.

Does it stand for someone's initials, or does this person know Jack well enough to presume he'll know them instantly?

The text thread reads:

*O.M.*

*I know you asked me never to contact you, but I love and miss you.*

*J.C.*

*Why are you reaching out to me now after all this time?*

*O.M.*

*Please, Jack! Our chance encounter made me realize I love you too much to walk away forever. Can I see you?*


*J.C.*
*Let me think about it.*


You bet I'm shocked.

And upset.

But I'm also fascinated. Who is she? How does Jack know her?

How recently did they see each other after all this time?

And then it hits me: she was the contact's accomplice.

Why does Jack's knowledge of her involvement merit Top Secret clearance? Is it because of Jack's history with her that Ryan wants Jack to keep it from the rest of us—

Including me?

I put the PlayDoh disk in a ZipLock baggie and hide it in my recipe book—

And then I sniff the air: my pies are burning!

I run to the oven, but I'm too late. The crusts are black.

I grab the kitchen mitts and fling open the oven. One by one, I toss the pies in the sink.

I scrape all eight of my Fitz & Floyd French porcelain pie plates of their burnt offerings.

After they've cooled, I started all over again.

The sun is rising as I stumble into bed.

# 4

# Your Seating Arrangement

*The moment all invitations to your feast are RSVPed, you'll lay out the most crucial battle map of the year:*

*Where your guests will sit.*

*If you think I'm kidding and that you'll throw caution to the wind—that open seating can't be all that bad—I have two words for you: Quelle horreur! In fact, who ends up beside whom determines the success of your event. Here are the rules:*

***First, call for détente between warring parties.*** *Considering how long and hard you worked on the meal, the airing of long-held grudges at your dinner table will leave the worst aftertaste. Don't invite guests who can't bury the hatchet before slicing the turkey.*

***Next: Don't tempt fate.*** *In other words, don't put a Capulet next to a Montague, a Hatfield next to a McCoy, or a Ferengi next to a Klingon. (If none of these references ring a bell, diplomacy isn't the only thing you need to be schooled in.)*

***And finally, should war break out, make sure the peaceniks are seated far behind the demilitarized zone.*** *No one's nose should get bent out of the joint because they feel they are at the wrong end of the table. Which is the "wrong end?" Why, the one in which you've corralled the innuendo-inappropriate brother-in-law, the deaf-but-loud-trash-talking aunt, the addled grandpa, the snobby sister-in-law, and all unruly brats.*

*Before you ask if equanimity can be accomplished by buying a round table, I can assure you it won't. Let's face it: you'll still have to look at those deemed inappropriate. Why chance a tummy ache when you eventually overhear them say something egregious? You know what they say: absence makes the heart grow fonder. (And it beats buying a few more leaves for your table.)*

*Is there a chance that one or more of the banished will realize they've been placed in Thanksgiving's equivalent of Siberia? Perhaps. But what's the worst that can happen—having them storm off and never seeing them again?*

*If so, you can thank me later—with chocolate.*

---

I HEAR VOICES...

But not here in the bedroom:

Downstairs.

I reach out to see if whoever it is has awakened Jack as well—

But I feel nothing.

Is he downstairs, too?

*What time is it?*

I force an eye to open and stare at my bedstand clock—

Oh my God—it's *almost noon*!

I leap out of bed, propelled by all that I still must do in the next forty-eight hours: the silver, the table linens—

And the crystal and fine china! Will there be enough pieces that match?

My ears finally tune into the voices coming from downstairs. Yes, I hear Jack. And the other is...

*Lee?*

I can't make out what they're saying, but their voices are strident.

Ah, heck! I better get down there before "strident" becomes "angry."

Or worse yet, someone decides to throw a punch.

That someone being Jack. Punching out a former POTUS can get you imprisoned for life. I hope he remembers that the ride from here to the closest supermax facility is a long one for his loved ones. And despite our stellar record for covertly keeping terrorists at bay, there's no guarantee that our current POTUS, Libby Kentfield would pardon him, especially after he was caught on her Secret Service team's wire wondering aloud if she cheated at poker. Or, as he put it: "Being a card counter, it takes one to know one."

I toss a robe over my jammies, grab my cell, and run to the stairs—

Just as my phone buzzes. It's a text from Mary. Startled, I trip on a step—

And go tumbling down the staircase.

By the time I hit bottom, the men are there too. Each grabs an arm and helps me to my feet.

"Are you okay?" The concern in Jack's voice only deepens the guilt creeping up my neck.

"Yes! ... I mean...I'm so far behind with food prep..." I shift my gaze to Lee. Forcing a smile, I add, "Sorry to have scared you."

"Ah! Well, now I feel silly bringing this up..." Lee's voice trails off.

"Bringing what up? Don't be shy." At this point, I'll say anything to change the conversation.

"Trisha invited us to your Thanksgiving shindig. Before I give Janie my answer, I want to ensure you—and Jack, of course—approve." He glances at Jack, whose face is as placid as an iced-over lake.

*Ouch.*

It's only been a few months since Jack's jealousy over Lee's infatuation with me was finally confronted—and resolved. Though I've made it perfectly clear to Lee that I'd prefer he move on from his unrequited love for me for years, Jack isn't convinced Lee can do that.

Since then, Janie, Trisha, and Jeff have stayed as thick as thieves. As for Lee, he's has made himself scarce. I hope that, like me, Jack has taken that as a sign that he has licked his wounds and, hopefully, moved on.

Which is why I'll be damned if I say yes, and damned if I don't. I know one way out of it: "Jack is in charge of the guest list."

"My vote? The more the merrier," Jack declares.

Shocked, I take a step backward—

Not a smart move since I trip on the step behind me. At least I end up sitting down, as opposed to falling on my ass.

"Ah! Well then..." Lee looks down at his feet. "My next question is, what time is dinner served?"

I stammer, "Say, three-ish?"

Lee smiles. "Then three-ish it is." He clenches Jack's shoulder and heads out.

When Lee opens our front door, I notice it's guarded by two of his Secret Service detail. One is Aunt Phyllis's husband, Porter Crosby. Porter glances my way, sees me, and winks.

I give him a thumbs up —

And wait until the door shuts before groaning at the memory of Aunt Phyllis's traditional contributions to our Thanksgiving groaning board:

A Jello mold.

My muffled outcry has Jack exclaiming, "Babe, what's wrong? Did you sprain something when you fell?"

"No... It's just that... Seeing Porter, it hit me that Aunt Phyllis will be making one of her Jello monstrosities."

Jack rolls his eyes. "Any warning as to what it will be this time? Frankly, I thought last year's was a new low. I mean, come on already! A Waldorf Salad Jello Mold?" He opens his mouth and sticks in a finger.

I can't blame him since it's my thought exactly. "This year's offering makes that one look sane."

Jack frowns. "Do I really want to know why?"

"Let me put it this way: it'll be a good waste of a meat you're usually fond of." I shudder. "At least I talked her out of adding gravy, too."

"This year, if Phyllis asks if we want the leftovers, don't be so polite," he warns.

"Give me some credit. I buried it in the backyard when she was out of the house."

"Only to have Lassie and Rin Tin Tin dig it up—and barf it all over my freshly cut lawn," Jack reminds me.

"Yes, well, what can I say? Our dogs have discriminating taste." I let him chuckle—

But I'm not letting him off the hook that quickly. "It was mighty gracious of you to invite Lee to Thanksgiving."

I feel Jack watching me out of the corner of his eye. If he's expecting me to give him a reason to be jealous again, he's got another think coming.

Finally, he grins. "You should have seen your face!" He tweaks my nose. "Let me guess: you thought we were fighting over you—again."

"I thought no such thing!"

"You're such a pretty little liar."

"I'm not lying, and you know it," I huff. My blush shows otherwise. To change the subject, I add, "Frankly, I was relieved to hear your quick—and genuine—response to his humble request."

Jack roars with laughter. "Listen to you, waxing poetically!"

It's the first time he's enjoyed anything since he got

called on the carpet by Ryan for botching our most recent mission. Hopefully, he can put it behind him.

Too bad it's at my expense.

Still, to extend this mood, I give him a long, soulful kiss—

But not as long as either of us would like because Jack's and my cells ping.

Really two for me: one from Ryan and one from Mary.

I'm about to read Mary's when Jack shows me what Ryan wrote:

## CLEAN UP ON AISLE 1

It's Ryan's way of letting us know to drop what we're doing and get into the office—like now.

On the Tuesday before Thanksgiving?

*Ah, heck.*

TO SAY that traffic on the 405 is more crowded than usual is an understatement. The busiest day of the year to fly is today.

But as we pass the exit to Los Angeles International Airport, I notice no planes are flying in or out. Since the sky is clear and blue, I'm surprised.

"There must be bad weather happening in other parts of

the country because LAX's air traffic is non-existent," I point out to Jack. "Do you think that has something to do with Ryan's emergency?"

"We'll find out when we get to Acme," he responds.

When we arrive, Arnie greets us at the door. "Let me have your cells," he says. "It's a safety precaution. Everyone must do it." Jack and I glance at each other, but we do as we're asked.

Dominic and Abu are already in the conference room, as is Emma, who has brought four-year-old Nicky. I'm not surprised that she and Arnie couldn't get a babysitter on such short notice. He's under the conference room table: a smart move on his parents' part since they won't want Ryan to see him. Tit for tat: Nicky wears earbuds to ensure he doesn't hear the swear words that are sure to come out of Ryan's mouth.

"What's he listening to?" I ask Emma.

"Anything is better than one of Ryan's colorful explosions, right?" Emma shrugs. "It's a talk about bugs. It's his new obsession."

She points to his coloring book, which is about insects. Nicky is intensely quiet as he scribbles on a praying mantis. I'm impressed that he's staying so well within the lines, albeit his bug is more colorful on the page than in real life.

Nicky doesn't even look up when Arnie and Ryan enter the room. However, Dominic certainly does because they have MI6 agent Teddy Twala with them.

That's to be expected since they have a personal history. Considering that just forty-eight hours ago, he was upset that Jody was out of town, this proves my theory about our British operative: he is an any-port-in-a-storm kind of guy.

"First, the good news. Acme's morgue team extracted the hard wallet containing Barry Telford's fee," Ryan proclaims. "Now for some bad news: all funds were transferred elsewhere—to a Cayman Islands offshore account." Ryan shows his disappointment with a scowl. "Knowing they'd kill Telford anyway may have made it a moot point to keep it in there. The even worse news: although we're doing everything to trace it to its final destination, having failed at the original mission, Acme won't be compensated anyway."

In other words, no bonuses for our team.

"And there's more bad news," Ryan continues. "The passcode to purge the malware has yet to be deciphered." He turns to Teddy. "As to its potential danger, MI6 operative Teddy Twala is here to personally deliver this intel from her agency's chief." He nods for her to speak.

"Our agency intercepted chatter from the Syrians regarding a plan that will blow up every U.S. domestic plane flying today," Teddy explains.

I ask, "With onboard suicide bombers? And if so, were they arrested?"

She shakes her head. "The plan doesn't call for any terrorists to actually board the planes. Instead, the passengers' cell phones can potentially kill them."

"How is that possible?" Dominic asks.

"Via the same data interception, MI6 learned that years ago that, at Russia's behest, Syria planted operatives in the microchip companies that supply the world's largest mobile device manufacturers," Teddy explains. "The malware-embedded microchips were in shipments of cellular phones distributed to the United States."

"Let me guess. The SD card used in Barry Telford's brush pass held the passcode that would initiate the trojan in the mobile devices," I deduce.

"Go to the head of the class," Ryan replies. "Telford did indeed worked for the American microchip company. He also acted as the company's liaison with its overseas manufacturing plants."

"In other words, he was in the perfect position to have the chips embedded with a trojan that can be activated when the passcode is texted to it," Jack reasons, "which turns it into a nano-bomb."

"So, that's why no planes are flying today!" I exclaim.

Arnie lets loose with a whistle. "And with today being the largest travel day, there's no better time to set off an incident of mass terror."

"Exactly. For everyone's safety, President Kentfield grounded all flights," Ryan explains. "She has also ordered all cell phone service to be discontinued until we catch Telford's contacts."

"Despite heading off a massive act of terrorism on U.S. soil on a beloved holiday, I presume it hasn't endeared her to the American public," Dominic chimes in.

"You're right," Ryan concedes. "However, she's put into place a few work-arounds. For example, starting immediately, the National Guard will be involved in the confiscation of the cellular devices and the immediate replacement of their microchips. POTUS will address the nation with her full plan in the coming hour."

"Considering that this national emergency is occurring over a seven-day travel holiday, I'd hope so," Abu adds.

"There is one bit of good news," Ryan continues. "The embedded chips aren't in cell phones procured for U.S. military personnel, which includes Acme-issued devices. Still, having initiated our agency's precautionary measures, Arnie will now give them back to you. In the meantime, Acme's prime objective is to find Telford's contacts."

"Do you think they're still in the area?" Abu asks.

"That depends on their marching orders from Russia. If the goal was to initiate the largest terrorist act on U.S. soil since 911, the mission should be considered aborted," Ryan points out. "But that doesn't stop Russia from trying it another day or another way. So yes, they may not have left."

"The travel embargo would have stranded them too," Arnie points out.

"Since Jack IDed the perpetrators, he can pass along their names and descriptions to local law enforcement," I suggest.

"Taken care of," Jack replies. "In fact, they've been sighted locally. It's only a matter of time before they're in custody."

I must ask: "So, who are they?"

"Mrs. Craig, until they're in custody, that information is still classified." Ryan's tone warns me not to ask again.

Teddy can't hide her smirk.

I'd stick out my tongue, but I don't because I'm a much bigger person.

Not to mention, Ryan is still giving me the stink-eye.

Finally, he stands up. "Meeting adjourned. Ms. Twala, please follow me so I can debrief you on another topic."

As I start out the door, Dominic taps my shoulder. "I say, old girl: I take it you'll have no objection if Teddy accompanies me to your soiree?"

I huff, "Considering you want a favor, calling me 'old girl' is not the best way to get it."

He hangs his head. "Well, then... If you object—"

I sigh. "I don't. You know what they say: the more, the merrier."

"That's the spirit!" He chucks me under the chin. "And to honor the occasion, I'll bring an extra fruit cake!"

I shake my head. "Just bring more brandy, okay?"

If this party gets any bigger, I'll need more booze.

Not for the guests but for my private pity party afterward.

# 5

# Naughty Auntie

*There's one in every family, right?*

*You know who she is:*

*She can be any age, but in her mind, she's just turned twenty-one and parties that way.*

*If you're a teen and want a sip of her cocktail, she first pours it into a water glass so you won't get caught and tells you to drink up.*

*For that matter, if she catches you smoking—anything— she chides you for not sharing and then takes a puff.*

*In her mind, she's still your age. That's why when you come to her with an issue that you wouldn't dare ask your parents, her answer—yes or no—will be bluntly honest and from the heart.*

*So yeah, listen to her. She's been there, done that, and likely gotten caught.*

*Or, to paraphrase Oliver Wendell Holmes Sr., "The young*

*woman knows the rules, but the old woman knows the exception."*

---

WE MAKE it home just a few minutes before all television networks broadcast President Libby Kentfield's speech. Anxiety is etched on Jeff and Trisha's faces as they stare silently at our great room's monitor, waiting for it to begin.

Although it seems like forever, it's only a few minutes before all network anchor chatter is hushed and the presidential seal is replaced by President Kentfield standing behind a podium with a row of American flags at her back. Because the public has long ago embraced her warm smiles, folksy manner, and the nickname bestowed on her by the press—"America's Favorite Aunt"—her stoic demeanor leaves little doubt that what she has to say is as dire as it is vital.

She is silent for the first few seconds. Then:

"My fellow Americans, today, an allied country intercepted a missive from a hostile nation revealing that the two civil liberties we hold near and dear—American democracy and freedom—are being threatened." At this point, Libby takes a deep breath. "Once again, terrorists planned to blow up the flights of those who were traveling to spend this beloved holiday week with family and friends. In response, as of three A.M. today, I grounded all incoming and outgoing airline flights."

After letting this sink in, Libby continues: "The terrorists' modus operandi wasn't to board the planes. Instead, while in the air, all passengers with cell phones purchased in the United States would receive a particular text message, seemingly from their airline. If they were to respond, a nano-bomb embedded in the phones' CPU—that is, its Central Processing Unit—would explode. Knowing this, I also ordered all phone companies to cease cellular communication nationwide. The cellular towers will stay dark until our country is out of danger. Additionally, military personnel are removing all passengers' and flight staff's infected microchips. Those citizens who have stayed home for the holiday will be visited by National Guard units to collect the infected chips from your cellular devices. In the same manner, safe chips will eventually replace them." She pauses again before adding: "As for land lines, since they are connected via ethernet cables, they are not affected. For those Americans who do not have a landline, every community already serviced by public facilities with multiple land-lines will stay open so local citizens can use their phones to connect with their loved ones." Libby takes a deep breath. "As to what our country will do going forward: first of all, our country's chip makers and telecom companies have already agreed to manufacture their products in stateside facilities. Also, these products will be subject to stringent quality assurance by our government's cybersecurity division. As for this particular terrorist act, one traitor was killed while being apprehended for his role in the plot. However, two other would-be terrorists are still at large. Despite having no known photos, their names are on the INTERPOL's

Red Notice."

The camera moves in on Libby: "Though we are a nation with unmatched economic power and military might, a terrorist act strikes at the very heart, soul, and spirit of our nation. However, we cannot allow it to evolve into a crisis of confidence. We cannot let fear undermine our collective unity of purpose for our nation. We cannot let today's incident erode—or worse, *destroy*—the social fabric of America. As of now, less than forty-eight hours before the American holiday that celebrates friendship as much as it does family, let us give thanks that we have allied countries that have our backs, as well as a strong, well-trained, and well-armed military that has proven, time and again, it can pivot with strength, ingenuity, and speed on any battlefield —even in cyberspace." Nodding, she adds, "My fellow Americans, I wish you a safe and peaceful Thanksgiving."

The screen dissolves into the presidential seal before cutting away to the network's news team for its analysis.

I exclaim, "Wow! She pretty much covered all the bases."

Trisha nods. "Had even one bomb gone off, it could have been horrible!"

Jeff's eyes shift to Jack and me. "She did a great job placating the American public, but something tells me that's not the whole story."

Jack shrugs. "You're right. It shows you've been around us long enough to understand that some things are better left unsaid."

"Besides not knowing the whereabouts of the other two accomplices?" Our son asks.

"Unfortunately, yes," Jack admits.

With a sigh, Jeff pulls his mobile from his jeans pocket and tosses it onto the kitchen table. "I guess I don't need to tote this around for the time being."

It dawns on me: "We also have a land line. Remember? It's in the kitchen. The number is on the fridge. If your friends need to reach you, give them that. If no one pics up, the call will go to voicemail."

"Does Mary have the number too? If not, she and Evan should, in case she has an emergency on the way home from Berkeley," Jack reminds me.

Suddenly, I feel guilty for not having returned Mary's texts. "I'm going to call Mary's counselor—and Evan's too—and remind them of the land line's number. I also want them to know that if no one picks up, they're to leave a message in voice mail."

Trisha laughs. "It's just like the Stone Age, when Mom and Dad grew up!"

"Hey, wait a minute! We aren't *that* old," I insist.

Jeff raises a brow. "Do you mean to tell me you had texting back in the day?"

Jack guffaws. "I'll have you know that mobile phones have been around since the 1970s, albeit they weren't as 'smart' as they are now. They weighed a ton too—several pounds, in fact."

Trisha snickers. "Another reason why guys in your generation wore their jeans below their waists."

"Now, that's a fashion trend I'd wish away forever," I mutter. I pick up a canvas book bag. "Okay, folks, toss your phones in here. Should the National Guard come looking for them ,I'll leave this bag in the garage."

Trisha perks up. "Oh, Mom—I forgot to tell you! Aunt Phyllis was looking for you."

"Did she say what it's about?"

"She wants your opinion on which Jello mold she should bring on Thanksgiving."

Jack's gagging sounds earn him an elbow to his side. "I'm starting my side dishes. I'll call her and ask her to come here."

Trisha shakes her head. "She asked that you go to Lion's Lair instead. She's teaching Janie and me how to make her favorite traditional Thanksgiving dish."

Jack and I turn to stare at each other. Then, in unison, we declare, "You're kidding...right?"

Trisha sighs. "If only I were!"

I give her a hug. "We can head up the hill together." To Jack, I ask, "Want to join us?"

He shakes his head. "Are you kidding? One Jello mold a year is enough for me. Do us all a favor and try to talk her out of it."

"Okay. I'll be back as soon as I can."

"No need to rush. I think I'll go for a run instead." He kisses my forehead. "Maybe this break from communication means society will slow down for a while. Better yet, maybe the country should consider making it another Thanksgiving tradition. You know, tuning out everyone and anything we can't see, hear, taste, smell, or feel one-on-one."

"You mean, go analog?" I chuckle. "I wouldn't mind

that a bit."

"Agreed." Jack's eyes are pierced with sadness.

Is he regretting having responded to the mysterious O.M.?

At least for now, she'll no longer be able to text him.

And he can't text back.

I wave as I head out the door.

---

DESPITE THE CELL PHONE BLACKOUT, Lion's Lair is a beehive of activity—not unusual. Since Lee's forced retirement from being the President of the United States, he's thrown himself into raising his two children and growing the success of his charities. Having made his fortune as a venture capitalist, he realizes this is the best way to give back to the world.

He's right.

After Trisha and I have been cleared to enter Hilldale's grandest estate, Janie joins us on the trek to the cottage that Aunt Phyllis shares with her husband, Porter Crosby, who is also the senior officer on Lee's Secret Service detail.

Just as I knock on the door, I get yet another text from Mary. I'm about to read it, but then Aunt Phyllis flings open the door and pulls Trisha and me in for a group hug. "Your timing couldn't be better!"

"Oh? Why's that?"

"Because I've got a great surprise for you! While I grab some plates and spoons from the kitchen, head on into the dining room." She shoos us in that direction—

Where we find three Jello molds.

The girls' queasy looks speak volumes. I ask, "Are you two alright?"

"We...just need some fresh air!" Janie declares. "Enjoy your taste test!" She's out the back door in a flash.

As Trisha scurries after her, she mutters, "I think this so-called cooking lesson has cured me of my career dream to be a chef."

*Yikes.*

Aunt Phyllis comes back with some of her vintage Fiesta Ware dessert plates. When she sees I'm alone, she asks, "What happened to the girls?"

"They...um... went to check on Harrison." Time to change the subject—and fast. "Gee, Aunt Phyllis, I don't know what to say...except that you...you've...outdone yourself!"

"I know! Haven't I? It's going to be the best Thanksgiving ever!" Her eyes sparkle with pride. "I heard this year will be a full house, what with the Chiffrays and everyone from the office—"

"Well, not exactly everyone. Ryan won't be there...So maybe you should keep one here for you and Porter."

"Oh, pshaw, missy! Frankly, since Porter is my official taste tester, I just know he's already had his fill of Jello for the year." She shrugs. "As for Ryan—well, let's face it, he won't be missed, especially since that Grumpy Gus never struck me as the 'Jello mold' type."

"What do you mean by that?"

"He's too much of a food snob."

If he's a snob, what does that make the rest of us?

Sheesh! If only she knew how many of my monogrammed cloth napkins have been ruined when she turns her back, and my family and I spit out red, green, or the gravy-colored globs that embalm her colorful meat treats?

But I digress. "So, tell me, Aunt Phyllis, what exactly is a 'Jello mold type?'"

"Why, we foodies, of course! You know—connoisseurs with exquisite taste and creative souls—especially when tying on the food bag, am I right?" She wraps an arm around my waist. "I thought you might be too busy to come here before the big day. I'm glad to see all the rigamarole about the cell phone blackout has lightened your load somewhat—"

*Ha! If only she knew!*

"—because I made mini-molds for you to taste them first. And if you like one or two especially, I'll make even more!"

"Seriously, Aunt Phyllis, that isn't necessary—"

Before I can stop her, she shoves a spoonful of the olive, carrot, and kiwi mold into it.

If I don't swallow it, I'll choke to death—

And, after all my mission drama, there ain't no way I'll die *that* way.

I make myself gulp down the chunky salty goo. When I'm sure I won't upchuck it, I raise my lips into a smile. "Yummy! Yep, that's a keeper, for sure."

"I'm so relieved you think so! After Porter's reaction, I

thought I'd have to toss it. Now for the next one—"

I'm saved by the bell. Well, the front door buzzer, anyway. Aunt Phyllis glances down the hall. "Ah! It's Eve! I wonder if she'd like a few bites too?" Phyllis goes to the door to usher in Lee's secretary.

No, she's much more than that. Besides being his Girl Friday, she's in love with him.

Why can't he see that? He did once—but blew it by allowing her to be swept off her feet by another guy.

Make that a cad. And an asshole. And worse yet, world chess champion Mason Ledbetter was a long-embedded Russian asset who kidnapped me to torture and sell to Russia so that it could trade me for one of its spies captured stateside.

Ah, good times.

When Eve came to her senses, Lee was waiting for her.

Sadly, Eve is like the rest of us: once burned, twice shy.

It doesn't help that Lee has made no bones that he sees me as his ideal woman. It took me declaring point-blank that Jack was the only man I could love for Lee to finally get the message: he may be rich, handsome, and kind, but he isn't the man who has saved me time and time again—from myself, and from every terrorist who has tried to bury me six feet under. (One, quite literally.)

Lee has now come to accept that Jack is the only person I love and ever will.

And now Eve, the woman who once loved Lee unconditionally, is again within his reach in this fifty-acre estate on its own hilltop, which boasts a forty-three-room mansion and an eighteen-hole golf course.

She kisses Phyllis's cheek. Her fondness for Porter has endeared my aunt to her. Eve's challenge now is to sweetly and politely turn down Phyllis's insistence that she join our taste test. I credit her for choosing a little white lie: "If only I could! I've just had my lunch—a power drink—because I'm fasting for the big day. And, alas, when Lee heard that Donna was on the property, he had to say hello."

Yikes. I had hoped to slip in and out without his knowing. Ah well.

Phyllis can't counter that either. Instead, she chucks Eve under the chin and then does the same to me before seeing us to the door.

I wait until we're out of earshot before saying, "Thanks for saving her feelings and me from a stomach pump."

Eve laughs. "I think it's sweet how Porter is too gaga over her to tell her how much he hates her Jello concoctions. I guess it's true that love is blind." Her smile fades. "I know it firsthand."

"Mason is in the rearview mirror," I remind her.

I want to add, *and Lee is right in front of you,* but that's not subtle enough for a woman with a broken heart. "By the way, you're also invited to Thanksgiving. But please don't feel you have to bring anything. There will be so much food as it is—"

"It's kind of you, Donna, to think of me, but...well, with all that's happening, someone has to man the fort. The cell phone blackout makes me the point guard should President Kentfield need Lee's shoulder to cry on."

"Frankly, I thought she handled it brilliantly. She sounded knowledgeable, reassuring, and in charge."

"Things aren't always what they seem."

"What do you mean?"

"Just that—" Eve stops mid-sentence. "Ah, Lee is waiting for us at the door. Let's pick up this conversation another time."

"Gotcha."

Is she worried that his feelings for me are still strong?

It's too late to ask. In a few strides, we're face to face with Lee.

Eve watches as he gives me a hello kiss.

Did she notice he lingered a bit too long?

If so, her placid smile doesn't slip.

I want to slap them silly and yell that life is too short and precious to play games with those we love. Instead, I walk in lockstep with them, regaling them with my pie fiasco story and promising Eve I'll save her a piece of each one.

This time, she doesn't mention her faux diet. I'm glad. I guess she doesn't hate me after all.

And yet, her upper lip quivers when Lee proclaims, "Thanks, Eve. I can take it from here."

Putting his hand on the small of my back, he steers me into his study, firmly shutting the door behind us.

But not before I see Eve's face, especially the sadness in her eyes.

Lee steers me to one of the leather sofas that face each other across a large coffee table. Instead of moving behind his desk, he sits beside me.

He's yet to let go of my hand.

The minutes seem to mount up before he finally says, "I promised myself I'd never put you in an awkward position again, especially regarding... well, regarding my feelings."

*Aw, heck. Here it comes...*

"I just have one request," he continues, "and then I'll... I'll never ask anything of you again. I promise."

"Lee, I really don't think you should—"

"Please just... just hear me out, Donna!" His voice aches with desperation.

"Okay, Lee. What is it?" I close my eyes, bracing for the worst—yet another declaration of his love.

# 6

# Crystal Clear

*Those of us with expensive crystal kept in a cabinet that only sees the light of day during rare occasions have experienced the disappointment of finding this special glassware in worse shape than we last remembered. We whine under our breath, "How could that be?"*

*Well, let me tell you:*

***First, don't leave your crystal on an open cabinet or display shelf.*** *Whether you like it or not, dust is in the air. Solution: After washing, dry thoroughly and put it in a cabinet that can be closed. If it has glass doors, all the better to display your beautiful collection.*

***Next, don't put your crystal in the dishwasher.*** *The reasons are many. For example, something can move during the wash cycle, increasing the chance that it will be broken. (I speak from experience!) Also, if you pull it out before it's completely dry, you'll find water spots that must be rinsed* *away anyway. Solution: Wash by hand, dry by hand, and check for water spots before putting them in a closed cabinet.*

***And finally, if you've done all of this but still find the glasses smudged, consider the obvious**—especially if you live with others. Perhaps one of your cohabitants is in the habit of tippling, but doesn't want you to catch on. Believe your eyes (when bottles disappear), your mouth (or they seem watered down), your nose (smell the suspect's breath), and your ears (their slurred words).*

*Solution: Lock the cabinets—to your fine china and to your liquor and wine.*

*And then, hide the key.*

---

"I WANT to bring a plus one to your Thanksgiving table." Lee glances away as if he's embarrassed for having asked.

"Oh...but of course!" Thank goodness! He's bringing Eve after all! 'Bout damn time he realized how lucky he is to have found someone as beautiful, kind, and savvy as the secretary who adores him. "Eve is always welcome."

Lee shrugs. "No, not Eve. A new...friend."

Well, bowl me over! When the cloud of shock and awe abates, I stammer, "Of course."

He nods his thanks. "Her name is Dina McMurtry. I really think you'll like her."

"I'm sure I will."

Hearing this, he smiles, relieved.

"How did you meet her?"

"She's a documentarian. She flew in on Monday to discuss producing a three-part series focusing on the success of our foundation. Each episode will walk viewers through the day-to-day workings of one or two of its specific programs. My foundation board has been urging me to do this for quite some time now, but I've held off."

"Why?"

He hesitates, then adds, "Because I didn't create the foundation to promote myself. It's always been my passion project, and I'm its public face. But the board—and Dina— is right. It must grow beyond me to accomplish its greater purpose: to be my legacy and that of Janie and Harrison. Dina has convinced me that we should play up the personal angle—not just that I'm a former president or that I built my success from scratch in the tech sector, but that the foundation is the best way to use my knowledge, money, and influence to make the world a better place."

"I'm glad she persuaded you to toot your own horn. It'll go a long way toward attracting donations."

Lee shrugs. "I hope so. It's the most important thing I'll leave my children. My goal is that they grow up to cherish it as much as I do."

"I'm sure they will, Lee. I look forward to hosting Dina." I pat his arm to reassure him that I'm happy for him, even if I'm sad that he doesn't see what his life may have been with Eve at his side.

"Her cameraman is here too. His name is James Gregg. He can eat his Thanksgiving meal with the household staff and those on my security detail who are off duty that day and stranded because of the travel embargo..." Lee's voice trails off in the hope that I catch his drift: that it wouldn't be too much to ask for James to join the rest of us.

I laugh. "Don't be silly. Despite the house already busting at the seams with unexpected guests, I'll have enough food to feed an army. And besides, neither Dina nor James planned on being stranded here."

"Yes...I mean, no! It's just... It's a sad reality that this terrorist act happened when they were here to take this meeting." Lee's face has turned red.

My God! Does this mean he's really smitten with this woman, Dina?

Lee is a fool. He doesn't know a good thing when it's right in front of his eyes: Eve.

Now, I'm curious to meet Dina and see for myself why his head was turned by their chance meeting.

Hopefully, the travel embargo won't push him to make rash decisions.

---

I PULL into our driveway to find my neighbor, Penelope Bing, sitting on my veranda with Jack.

He's got his shirt off. His chest and abs shine with sweat from his run.

That would be enough to keep my frenemy's hands from patting them, right? *Wrong.* Her hand moves downward from Jack's nipple toward his belly button.

But before it goes any further, I grab her wrist and

squeeze it hard. "As they say in all the best stores, 'Look, but don't touch.'"

Despite the pain causing her eyes to tear up, she giggles. "Is he for sale? Because I'll Venmo you right now."

"Save your money," I warn her, "because if that hand goes south of the Mason-Dixon line, it'll be too broken to pay for your hospital bill."

Penelope jerks her hand away. "I was just demonstrating a massage technique that is proven to stimulate the erogenous zones in the chest. It was taught to me by my new doctor."

"Is his name Hackenbush? Perhaps Hugo Z?"

Her mouth drops open. "Why... How did you know?"

"Hugo's reputation precedes him. Let's just say he's been around the block for eons." If she doesn't recognize the name of Groucho Marx's most famous character, that's on her, not me.

By now, Jack is laughing so hard that he's shaking.

"This block?" Penelope scowls. "Funny, you don't look like his type."

"Not to worry, Penelope. I'm a one-woman man." The knowledge puts her patented smirk back on her Collagen-plumped lips. "Where did you happen to meet this Hugo person?"

"He's my instructor for a course I'm taking—on tantric sex! I'll soon be offering a subscription of demonstrations through my shop's website."

Penelope's sex shop, Cum & Get It, is the talk of the town. Make that the town's laughingstock—especially when one of her dominatrix equipment demonstrations goes terribly wrong. Once, one of her johns—I mean "clients"— was electrocuted by a vibrator. Another time, she gagged and hogtied some guy in her "pink satin dungeon" (make that the store's basement) and forgot she'd left him there for three days. If passersby hadn't heard him moaning from his pain, she'd have been tried for enslavement. She was lucky that he was too embarrassed to press charges. But there are only so many warnings Hilldale's police department can issue for these little incidents before they finally end up with a murder on their hands.

By that I mean, if she doesn't kill some guy, his wife will kill her.

Oblivious to my own murderous tendencies toward this latest Jack attack, Penelope smiles seductively. "Of course, for the right price, I also offer live courses one-on-one."

By now, Jack is laughing so hard that he's doubled over and sputtering. When he finally catches his breath, he gasps, "Priceless!"

"Isn't it? I knew *you'd* appreciate it!" Her hand reaches out again to pet him—

But I slap it away just in time. "Other than getting yet another opportunity to be touchy-feely with my husband, why are you here?"

"To ask a teensy-tiny favor," Penelope pouts. "Doctor Hackenbush and I had planned a Thanksgiving getaway. The great news is my darling Cheever was released early from his unfortunate incarceration for that childish indiscretion. However, the bad news is that Hugo and I are still on the hook for our love cabin unless we find someone to watch over Cheever while we're away."

"'Childish indiscretion?'" I snicker. "Did you forget that he passed state secrets in coded messages to Russia via his FaceStaTweet influencer account?" Then it dawns on me: "How did he get out of prison?"

"He...We had an excellent attorney." Penelope shrugs.

"Let me guess. Cheever's sentence was reduced because he informed on his cellmate."

"Well, yes! ... And he agreed to wear an ankle bracelet for the rest of his sentence term," she admits. "But the only thing that matters is that my little boy is home with me!"

"Then stay home with him—*because he needs you.*"

"You don't get it! *I* need Dr. Hackenbush!" She tears up. "Look, Donna, we haven't always seen eye to eye. But considering all I've been through... I ... I really need to get away!" She turns to Jack. "You said she'd be kind!"

*Jack committed me to babysit Cheever so that she could play Pattycake with some hack-in-a-bush—*

Hers.

The nerve of him!

Realizing I'm close enough to hurt him, Jack backs away. "Penelope, Donna has a lot on her plate for the next few days. Here's a solution: if you give me the shock code for Cheever's ankle bracelet, I'll be his host for the weekend."

"Sold!" She leans in to whisper it.

And yes, I see that while one hand cups his ear, the other is back on his abs.

I don't have time for this. I fume into the house.

I WALK into the great room to find Jeff playing video games with Cheever—

Only Cheever doesn't have a controller in his hand.

Instead, he's cuddling one of my pies—

And his large stubby hands—sans fork—is ready to dig into it.

*Like hell, he will.*

I propel myself across the room—

And snatch the pie away before his fat, germ-infested fingers can claw into it. "How dare you!"

"But I'm STARVING! And besides, you got six others."

"No, I have eight."

"Not anymore." Cheever points to an empty pie dish. I can tell which one he ate from the cherry juice on his lips. "To be honest, it was worse than the crap I was served in the hoosegow! Even my mom can make a better pie—which says a lot."

It's bunk, and he knows it. "Then why were you cuddling the other one?"

"Hey, I'm doing you a favor! Trust me, you don't want to end up in jail for food poisoning."

Suddenly, I'm tempted to bake a special pie just for him, with cherries—

Poisonous pits and all.

Jack's reflection is on the television monitor as he sneaks behind me to go upstairs.

"My *husband*"— I emphasize Jack's position in my life

so that he knows that he can't miss my point, which is precarious at best—"has the shock code to your ankle bracelet. Should you touch one iota of food without my permission, I will personally hold his finger down on the damn button until you're as flaky as that crust. Am I making myself clear?"

Cheever nods.

Then he burps.

I'm at the end of my rope. It's time to have it out with Jack.

---

I ENTER our bedroom to find Jack stripping down to shower.

I'd love to do the same:

With him.

As if reading my mind, Jack rewards me with an impish grin. "Care to join me?"

I peek into the bathroom. "As long as Penelope isn't in there too—or has somehow embedded it with one of her webcams."

Jack roars with laughter. "I heard you were summoned to the Lord of Lion's Lair. What did he want?"

"To ask if he could bring a date." I watch my husband's face for a telltale sign of relief.

"Good! He's bringing Eve."

"I'd hope so too, but no. Apparently, Lee has a new lady friend."

"*Well, well, well*! I'm glad he's moved on—from you." Jack smirks. "I assume you made it be known that I'd welcome anyone he wishes to bring."

"As disappointed as I am that it's not Eve, I intend to welcome Lee's new lady friend with open arms."

"What say you open them for me instead?" He pulls me in close—

For a kiss.

And to unbutton my blouse.

Then to unclasp my bra.

He kneels down to toss off my shoes.

And then strips off my jeans.

When he tugs down my panties, he lifts one leg, then another, so that I can step out of them.

By now the bathroom is filled with the shower's hot steam. Jack's lips seek out mine as he carries me toward it.

---

DAMP: everything we touch: the tiled walls, the plush towels flung over the shower door, my eyes as Jack fiercely enters me.

Soaking wet: my hair, his broad firm back, my first orgasm.

Hot: the water, my dirty talk, Jack's piston-like thrusts in response to my guttural commands and pleas.

Empty: Us, after this long furious bout of sex. Alas, so is my shampoo dispenser.

Revived: Us, after Jack lovingly massages my hair with his shampoo, and I reciprocate in kind.

Of course he insists on showing me his thanks again—

And again.

Until there is no more hot water.

---

WHILE JACK SHAVES, I towel off, wrap myself in my robe, and move to the bedroom.

For the rest of the day I've vowed to shelve any conversation that will add additional stress to this day, this week, this terrorist situation, and the holy terror who's got his eyes on my pies and his grubby stubby fingers poised over them—

But then I notice a note peeking out from Jack's discarded jogging pants.

It doesn't have an envelope.

I pull it out and read it:

*Dear Jack,*

*Please find a way to break away again, even if it's just for a few minutes. If the loving bond we once shared in the past doesn't sway you, I promise—I'll make it worth your while.*

*— O.M.*

Through our open window, I hear our postman's off-key whistling. Today, it's the Carpenters' old hit, *Close to You.*

If it wasn't already in the mailbox, how did this O.M. person get this to him?

There's only one answer: she handed it to him when he met with her just now while he was supposedly out jogging—

*And she's already begging for another rendezvous.*

Will Jack be tempted again?

And if so, why?

7

## Table Settings

*An impressive table is only a good as its settings. No one says they have to be expensive (albeit that would be nice for those who memorize brands and price tags).*

*Nor must your centerpiece must be spectacular enough to impress the Met Gala's producer. (Though, admittedly, that would be FABULOUS!)*

*Instead, strive for elegance and simplicity. Long tapered candles, perhaps? Their holders could be miniature pumpkins, providing your table with spots of orange. How about real leaves from neighboring trees for other bursts of the season's color? Consider Liquid Ash (purple), Gingkoes (yellows), and Maples (scarlet). Now that everyone on the block has raked them, you have plenty of piles to hunt for ones in the right hues—*

*And, if the piles are large enough, they are the perfect place to hide a dead body.*

*Tip: place it deep within the heap so that, when the bonfire is lit, there's no telltale sign of it when it goes up in smoke.*

---

"MOM?... *MOM! COME IN HERE, NOW!*"

It's eleven on Wednesday morning, and I've got my hands deep in the dough that will be used for the lattice top on the pie, replacing the one that ended up in that bottomless pit that is Cheever Bing's belly.

To ensure no other Cheever raids on my Thanksgiving meal before the T-Day Countdown in less than fifteen hours, all dishes are padlocked in the extra refrigerator kept in our garage. The seven previously baked pies are hidden in a secret kitchen pantry that also holds enough munitions to fight off a battalion. It's just one of the redesigns to our home that occurred after it was blown to Kingdom Come— by us, to obliterate any incriminating evidence before a totally uncalled-for FBI raid commenced.

Again, I digress.

My sigh comes from my lack of sleep. Jack's light snoring wasn't the reason. It's knowing he is covertly communicating with some old girlfriend.

Still, I rouse myself and glance into the great room to see what all the commotion is about:

In a voice that would make a funeral director proud, a TV announcer says: "We interrupt this regularly scheduled program for this special news bulletin. A few minutes ago, on TikTok, an anonymous source uploaded video footage of President Libby Kentfield caught in what is known in broadcasting as a 'hot mic' moment. By that, I mean her microphone was still live after her emergency telecast about the terrorist incident that has shut down all flights coming in and out of the United States, as well as all cell phone service."

As the announcer fades out, we see video footage of POTUS again. Because she's still at the podium and a few of her aides are approaching her, it seems to have occurred immediately after Libby's speech.

Upon hearing the broadcast's producer shout, "Cut! ..." Libby's stoic demeanor morphs into a cruel smirk. Three aides approach the podium: two females and a male. I recognize one of the women as the Senior Advisor to the President and the White House Communications Director, Jennifer Suarez. The man is the Deputy Assistant and Principal Deputy Director of Communications, Grant Federman. The other woman is Assistant to the President and the White House Press Secretary, Valerie Smith.

When Grant reaches up to help Libby step off the podium, we can't see his face, but we can hear him say, "I think lying to the American public is a big mistake—"

Libby slaps his hand away. "Zip it, asshole! I've got enough shit on my plate, what with the constant churn of *mérde* I already tell the American public. Whose idea was it anyway to pretend that quote-unquote terrorists have hacked everyone's phone and to blow everyone up on the biggest holiday travel weekend?"

"But...But... It was *your* idea, Madame President!" Jennifer's voice trembles.

"You said it was perfectly timed for your re-election next year—" Valerie adds.

"I stand firm what I said about using the original draft," Lawrence insists. "If you'd just told the American public the truth—that this administration can't make the cell service providers fix this tech glitch anytime soon—we might actually win your re-election despite this fuck-up."

Libby is so angry that she shakes. Shoving past him, she growls, "Bullshit! Average Joe and Jane America can't handle the truth! Line up calls with the cell phone providers and airlines. I want to ream them out for even suggesting we call off this hoax. Better yet, they better pony up with some big re-election donations if they don't want the cat to get out of the bag—"

The video cuts off.

*WOW*!

If Libby just admitted to deceiving the American public to enhance her re-election chances, the political and legal repercussions will be devastating.

I'm not surprised when my cell rings with Ryan's latest codeword:


## PILE-UP ON THE 405


My well-slept husband stumbles down the stairs. "Um... did you see..."

"About the 'pile-up?' Yep. And here's why." I point to

the television, where the network news is yet again replaying Libby's slip-up, along with their analysis of it.

Jack slaps his forehead. "What a shit show! I wonder if—"

"We better get going." I can tell he hears the curtness in my voice because he frowns, then shrugs to go back upstairs to dress into something besides his pajama bottoms.

If he were to ask me what's wrong, I would tell him that if he wishes to honor our pact—to be honest about our feelings for others—then now is the time to come clean about the mysterious O.M....

Yeah, right. I mean, who do I think I'm kidding?

I turn off the oven. My dough and filling go into our lockable refrigerator. I hope whatever news or mission Ryan has for us still leaves time for me to finish it before the meal tomorrow—

If there's going to be a meal at all.

---

BY THE TIME Jack and I walk through the conference room door, the rest of our team is already there, as is Teddy. She sits next to Dominic—so close that it's not hard to deduce that they are holding hands under the table.

Ryan is pacing the floor. His stare becomes an outright glare—at us—as we hurry to the two closest seats. Finally, he declares, "Acme has analyzed POTUS's hot mic incident."

"That's odd," Abu says. "Why isn't this being handled internally by the NSA?"

"Our NSA liaison, Mario Martinez, has made it clear that this request is at the behest of Director of National Intelligence Marcus Branham. Emma's intel analysis proves that DNI Branham's decision may make sense."

As Abu's eyes open wide, Ryan grunts his acknowledgment for Emma to begin.

She turns on the wall-sized monitor. "This is the original camera footage taken after the video feed ended."

It starts with the White House Communications producer saying, "And...*CUT*." Hearing this, Libby relaxes her stance while three aides approach the podium. Libby turns their way. Her calmness melts into a sad grimace and is accompanied by a shrug. Grant offers his hand to help her off the podium, and she takes it.

"How did I sound?" she asks.

"Assured," Jennifer says.

"In control," Valerie adds.

"At this point, the public knows the situation. And they know you have it under control," Grant declares.

Libby now smiles, relieved. As she heads off, she says, "I'll meet you back at the Oval. I've got to join the Joint Chiefs in the Situation Room—"

The video cuts off.

"Since we—and everyone else in the world—have all seen the TikTok version, we'll skip it," Ryan says. "Despite the White House putting out a press release declaring it a deep-fake and proving it with the original footage, the bogus version is still catnip to the broadcast news organizations."

"With cell and Wi-Fi access down in the U.S., how is this still making the rounds?" Dominic asks.

"That's easy," Arnie assures him. "Cable television can still be accessed without an internet connection. Coaxial or fiber-optic cables go directly from cable providers to subscribers' homes."

"Sadly, because this is the biggest news story of the year, the networks are going to milk it for all it's worth," Jack adds. "POTUS will have to do some extensive damage control."

"She's doing just that," Ryan admits. "In fact, I suggested that she contact Evan Martin's Black Tech for an assist."

Well, that has certainly gotten my attention.

"Good move," says Jack. "What is Acme's role in this?"

"We'll know more when Evan connects the dots," Ryan replies. "Like everyone else on the I-5, he's stuck in the state's biggest traffic jam."

I don't want to say it out loud because I don't want to manifest more chaos for the Family Craig, but I assume another fiasco will occur just when we're sitting down to Thanksgiving dinner.

Which means Evan and Mary may miss the meal altogether. As always, when it comes to our household, any act of terrorism takes precedence. I'm glad our kids love us despite this.

All the more reason I wish Evan and Mary weren't heading into this professional debris field.

Thank goodness Jeff, Trisha—and by proximity, Janie—are too young to get hurt by it.

---

JACK DOESN'T SPEAK on the ride home. Is he lost in thought?

And if so, are his thoughts about the mysterious O.M.?

To break the silence, I say, "Is there something that Ryan isn't telling us?"

Jack swerves too close to the next lane and gets blasted by the truck beside us. After we're far enough away from it, he glances over. "Now, why would you say something like that?"

"I don't know, exactly. It just seems this is coming at us in bits and pieces."

He snickers. "How is that different from any other mission we've had?"

"For some reason, it is." I shrug. "Maybe I'm just stressed, or fatigued, or something. But between the travel embargo, and the deepfake, and Thanksgiving now less than a day away—"

Jack takes my hand. "I don't want you to be worried about anything but Thanksgiving. And we're all here to help. Including me."

I lift his hand to my lips and kiss it. "Jack, it's kind of you to say. But... it's been obvious to me that your mind is elsewhere."

Jack drops his hand. "What makes you say that?"

Okay, here goes nothing...

Make that *everything:* "I know about... O.M."

Jack stops short. The car behind us slams on its brakes.

But apparently, the car behind it doesn't do the same because we hear a crash—

Which Jack avoids by speeding up and changing lanes—

And the car that was in front of us is now part of the fender bender.

"Jack—please! Slow down!"

"Don't change the subject. Have you been reading my texts?"

"How does it matter why or how I know about... about O.M.?"

"Because you're supposed to trust me, Donna! Or have you forgotten that?"

"No, of course, I haven't forgotten! And you're not supposed to keep secrets from me. Or have *you* forgotten *that?*"

"You're changing the subject!" he mutters.

"No—you are! Actually, you're projecting your guilt onto me!"

"And what exactly am I supposed to feel guilty about?" Jack shouts.

I shout back, "I don't know, Jack! Why don't you tell me what this O.M. person means to you?"

When he doesn't answer, I huff, "Unless...you're afraid to."

"Damn it, Donna! We'd finally reached a point where I felt I could trust you. And now..."

"Now what? What else am I supposed to think?"

His fuming goes on for the next two miles. Finally, he mutters, "Can we at least shelve this topic until after Thanksgiving? By then…it will be a moot issue."

*What the hell is that supposed to mean?*

That I've blown his trust yet again—and that this time, it's for good?

That I've given him the perfect excuse to walk out on me—

To her?

So much for trust, for clearing the air.

Worst. Thanksgiving. Ever.

# 8

# Polishing the Silver

*Before any event, you'll rest easier if all your table finery is spit-spot, especially your silverware. There are many non-toxic ways to polish it! Here's my favorite:*

*1. In a small bowl, mix simple baking soda and water into a paste: wet but not runny.*

*2. Rub the paste onto the tarnished silver with a clean, soft cloth.*

*3. Leave it on for about a minute. However, if it's heavily tarnished, you can gauge the length after three minutes and up to ten by rubbing off a little to see if the tarnish is disappearing.*

*4. Afterward, thoroughly rinse your silver with cool water, then dry it with another soft cloth. Check the nooks and crannies of your intricate pattern to ensure you get it all off.*

*5. The more you buff with the cloth, the more it will gleam!*

*6. By the way, silver cleaner is an excellent poison if you*

*need to eliminate "rats" (wink, wink, blink, blink) be they
animals or the human vermin species.*

---

I WAKE up at dawn with a start:

I'd forgotten to make any hors d'oeuvres!

But I've also forgotten to polish the silver.

I don't have time to do both unless I get up now.

*Darn, darn, darn.*

I turn to Jack's side of the bed—

Only he's not there. Did he go out for a run?

I don't want to think about who he may be running
into. Still, I'd like to know if there's some reason why he's
running away from me.

But now is not the time for a pity party, so I wipe
away my tears, leap out of bed, and stumble down the
stairs. At least I'll be too busy to think about Jack and
O.M.—

And from the looks of things, besides my health and the
happiness I share with my beloved family, I have yet another
thing to be thankful for today:

Jeff's distinctive signature scrawl is on a note sticking out
of the cabinet drawer holding my sterling silverware. It says:

**Happy Thanksgiving! I love you, Mom! —Jeff**

I open a drawer, pull out a fork, and hold it up to the
sunlight filtering through the drapes. No tarnish whatsoever.

It's the same with the antique silver tea service I inherited from my mother, who'd inherited it from hers.

What a boy!

No—now that he's a high school junior, I must face the fact that he's a young man.

And he's also an old soul. This random but thoughtful act of kindness proves it.

Ecstatic that I can now focus on the canapés, I open the locked pantry and refrigerator only to find that the provisions purchased to make them have been used to create an array of tasty appetizers. One glass-domed tray is filled with skewers of salty chorizo and briny olives. Another holds ploughman's nibbles, and a third is laden with pea and ham hock croustades. There are duck bites on cucumber squares drizzled with Hoisin sauce, and crispy sushi cakes topped with seared tuna. My favorite is the Swedish meatballs with Lingonberry sauce.

A note on one of the domes reads:

### *My Thanksgiving Day gift to the BEST MOM EVER! xoxox Trisha*

I love my kids.

I will gladly let them sleep in. They deserve it.

I go to the master bedroom to deck myself out as hostess with the mostess. To my surprise, Jack is singing in the shower. He must have slipped into the house while I was in the pantry. Instead, I head back to the kitchen, make a pot of coffee, and put out cereal and fruit for my family's breakfast.

By the time Jack dresses and comes downstairs, I've already eaten. I wave him over and give him a peck on the cheek like any other day. A quarter-hour later, Jeff and Trisha bound down the stairs. I throw my arms around them and whisper, "You are lifesavers. Thank you!"

Jack smiles benignly but isn't curious enough to ask what they did.

Yes, I am angry that he's too preoccupied to feel my angst and doesn't even care to ask what they did to deserve my praise.

And then I make myself a vow: that today I'll stay calm about him and this O.M. person. I don't need it ruining my favorite holiday.

All hell can break loose tomorrow.

———

AFTER I GET out of the shower, I take time to primp so that my makeup is flawless, and I've given myself an updo that would make Audrey Hepburn proud. I put on a new dress. It is short and casual yet chic: high-necked, pleated, and sleeveless. This trapeze dress boasts a black-and-white leafy print with a bow in the back.

Yep, I look as if I'm ready to party. If only I felt that way.

Jack and the kids are watching the Macy's Day parade. I've just pulled my mother's tea service from its glass cabinet and placed it on my sterling silver tray when Jack enters the dining room. Does he feel me stiffen when he puts his arms around me?

Since I can't—make that *refuse to*—show my feelings before we're inundated with guests, I force my lips into a smile. "Ah, you're just in time to stack the teacups and their saucers onto this tray. Afterward, you can put it on the dining room sideboard."

The doorbell rings with the first of our guests. "I'll get it. You just keep stacking."

"Ma'am, yes, ma'am," he says with a salute.

"That's the spirit!" I'm not joking. If we're to get through the next few hours, we'll need a sense of humor.

Our first guests are Arnie, Emma, and Nicky. By the time they walk inside, another car has pulled up. To my surprise, it's Evan's. He toots the horn.

Finally! I can't wait to hug them.

They must feel the same way because they don't even grab their bags before leaping out of the car. In a few steps I'm buried in a tight hug between them. "I'm so happy to see you both—now, more than ever," I say.

"But you've gotten my messages, right, Mom?" Anxiously, Mary takes my hand. "You're fine, right? I mean, with everything?"

"Yes...of course!" I stammer.

Is she talking about the meal? Or is she concerned about the terrorists? It certainly isn't about Jack and me—and the mysterious O.M.

After that long, exhausting drive, I certainly don't want to tell her about it.

"Oh...good!" Mary is all smiles again. "When you didn't answer, I thought... well, the worst—"

How can I admit to her that I never found the time to respond to her?

Besides, all is well because they are home now. Instead, I exclaim, "Oh, honey, I am so, so, sorry! No, it's all good—great, in fact! It's just that... you know... the terrorist attack—"

Dominic's ecstatic declaration—"Cheerio, Craigs!..." gets me off the hot seat. He and Teddy are already on the veranda steps. As promised, he's brought two bottles of sherry and his food offering: Lincolnshire plum bread.

"I'll open one of the bottles," he offers.

"Thanks. The aperitif glasses are on the side table in the dining room."

I usher everyone into the living room, where I'd already set up the bar: wines of all varietals, a full complement of liquors, an ice bucket, fruit, and syrups. Pretty in pink, Trisha places trays of canapés on the coffee table. Jeff, in a navy blazer, blue button-down shirt, and khaki slacks, accompanies her as she shakes Ryan and Carol's hands.

Behind them, Abu saunters up. He holds a covered dish in each hand.

"What goodies do we have here?" I ask.

"Kibbeh, which is lamb and bulgur wheat croquettes. Also, something for dessert: cashew baklava. I made both dishes myself."

"Sounds yummy! Feel free to put the kibbeh on the dining room sideboard with the other dishes, and I'll put the baklava with the desserts."

As I move in that direction, I pass Trisha, who is now

walking around the living room with a tray arrayed with many of her delectable appetizers. Jeff is following her lead. I've just placed Abu's baklava with the other desserts when the doorbell rings again.

Mary looks out the window. "Hey, guess who just showed up?"

Jack guffaws. "Don't leave us in suspense."

"It's Jody!"

Hearing this, I drop one of my mother's antique Dresden China teacups.

Thankfully, Jack catches it before it hits the floor.

As he hands it to me, I mutter, "If this keeps up, I'll have to beg Aunt Phyllis to bring her Fiesta Ware."

The doorbell rings. I go to answer it and give our unexpected guess a big hug, all the while thinking it should be interesting to see how Dominic reacts when he sees her.

Let's hope their reunion doesn't devolve into a food fight—or a murder: his—when the two loves of his life meet in the flesh.

"I hope you have room for one more guest," Jody says. "With the plane embargo and the cell towers down, I never had the chance to leave the country, and I couldn't text Dominic or you to tell you I was on my way."

"You're always welcome. Follow me."

From Jack's smirk, I can tell he's dying to come with us so that he doesn't miss the fireworks, but someone else must be coming down the walkway because he calls out with a cheery hello.

Dominic is holding court in the center of the room,

impressing others with his knowledge of sherries. Teddy is at his side. When Jody makes her entrance, Dominic's face loses all its color.

As Jody makes her way over, he drops his sherry glass.

Thankfully, Jeff is close enough to grab it. "A brilliant save if I do say so myself," Jeff declares.

I want to high-five him for keeping one of my mother's crystal glasses from shattering, but I'd prefer he move Dominic's glass to a safe place. Like, say, out of range of any catfight.

At first, Teddy is surprised. But as she follows Dominic's gaze, she realizes what is happening. The change in her face is minimal: only for a second does her smile quiver. As Jody walks over, Teddy steps forward and holds out her hand. "I'd hoped you'd show up."

"Ah! With me scheduled to be out of town, I thought you might be here," Jody busses her on both cheeks.

Dominic's jaw drops. "You...*you two know each other?*"

Jody rolls her eyes. "You've given us both keys to your bachelor pad, and you're out of town a lot. It was inevitable we'd run into each other."

"And compare notes," Teddy adds. "Now that we're all here together, you'll get to hear them."

Dominic gulps. "All stellar, I assume."

This sends his lady friends into fits of giggles.

The look on his face mirrors my thoughts:

*Boy, oh boy, it's going to be a hell of a night.*

The doorbell rings again. Realizing this, Jack has left his sentry post. I hurry to the front entry.

He does, too. But because he's still holding the tray of teacups, his hands are full.

I call out, "Don't worry, I'll get the door."

As Jack moves aside, I turn the knob. Janie bounds in, carrying a shopping bag. She gives me a quick kiss and a breathless "Happy Thanksgiving!" Holding up a the bag, she exclaims, "Party favors. They're like mine, but different colors!" She points to the hot pink Polaroid camera slung over her shoulder.

Aunt Phyllis, empty-handed, is right behind her. Seeing this, I must ask: "You didn't bring a Jello mold?"

She rolls her eyes. Jutting her chin at Porter, she declares, "Unfortunately, Mr. Fumble Fingers there dropped it. My best one, too—meatballs and gravy! But now it's in the middle of Lee's driveway, a feast for the ants and the ages."

Porter shrugs. As he walks in, Jack murmurs, "Thanks pal. We owe you one."

No kidding.

A second later, Jack's smile is gone. Lee has just stepped onto the verandah. He's got one hand centered on a beautiful woman's back: dark flowing hair, piercing green eyes, high cheekbones.

When she sees Jack, she gives him a knowing wink.

Jack looks down at the tray in his hand.

*What the heck is going on?*

Lee greets me with a hearty hello. "Donna, thank you for hosting us. I'd like to introduce you to... a new friend. Dina —that is, Ondine McMurtry—is the documentarian I mentioned." He then turns to the older man standing behind her. "And this is her cameraman, James Gregg."

*Ondine McMurtry...*

*O.M.*

No wonder Jack is rattled.

Ondine gives me a dismissive nod, but James holds out his hand. "Lee has had nothing but great things to say about you. I'm already a member of your fan club."

I turn my gaze to him. Silver-haired and more than twice my age, he holds himself straight. He's dressed casually but well: cashmere sweater over a button-down shirt, Saint Laurent slacks, Gucci loafers. But it's his eyes that render me speechless. They, too, are green and as mesmerizing as Ondine's. Taken aback, I murmur, "That's very kind of you to say. Welcome to our home. My husband, Jack..."

I turn to introduce them, but Jack is no longer there. Lee and Ondine are following him into the living room.

James laughs. "I guess the others have moved inside without us." Still holding my hand, he adds, "Shall we join the party?"

# 9

## Knives Out

A great carving knife serves three valuable functions: First, it is appropriately sized and balanced to cut to the desired thinness (or thickness, as the case may be).

Next, its razor sharpness ensures a mouth-watering slice of your crispy-skinned golden-brown turkey won't shred into unappetizing ribbons before being placed on your family's and guests' plates.

Finally, it serves as the perfect weapon to dismember any odious family members.

Helpful hint: Because of the amount of blood loss and the squeamishness it may cause, this third act should occur before the meal and out of the view of others. You wouldn't want your guests to lose their appetites, would you?

I EXCEL AT A CERTAIN SPYCRAFT: mindless but heartfelt chit-chat.

To pull it off, I hold another partygoer's gaze. All the while, this floater (that is, an unknowing asset) believes I'm avidly involved with our conversation. He may not know that whenever I open my mouth—to speak, to giggle, to duck modestly—it also allows me to scan the room.

Today, my guests give me additional cover because I'm also their hostess. As such, I'm allowed to glance away, nod, and smile at others or even subtly guide the person monopolizing my time to where I can best gather the intel I need.

I do this now with James. After asking where he originally hails from (Chicago) and how he got interested in documentary filmmaking (he's a New York University graduate, and "fiction doesn't interest me as much as facts that can make a difference in people's lives...") I finally ask the question that has been needling me for the last few days: "How does Ondine know my husband?"

James looks surprised. "He hasn't told you about her?"

I weigh how I should answer that. This once, honesty is the best policy. I shake my head. "No."

He lets that sink in. "You should ask him." Realizing he has stepped in *mérde*, he opts to clam up.

I can't say I blame him. No one wants to be the bearer of bad news because the messenger always gets shot.

In my case, it could be taken literally.

Apparently, James has caught onto that.

I have a good mind to prod an answer out of him, party be damned. But then I see Ondine is making her way over.

She waves—not to Lee or Jack.

To me.

I force a smile onto my lips—

But then I catch a glimpse of my face in the hall mirror. My lip gloss, now smeared from all my guest pecks, has morphed my smile into that of a jack-o-lantern's.

So be it.

She'll be lucky if I don't bite her.

---

"I'M SO sorry I haven't been able to break away before now, but Lee insisted on introducing me to everyone." Ondine's voice is as sultry as I'd expected—not just because she's a documentarian and, as such, does a lot of voiceover work on her films—

But because *she's a slut.*

That's not to say that all sluts sound the part. I've run into a few that would give Bronx streetwalkers a run for their money, not to mention several who could easily replace any Disneyland Minnie Mouse.

"That's okay." I reply. "It's allowed you to get reacquainted with Jack."

"Ah! ... Then...he's mentioned me?"

"Not previously. So go ahead and fill in the blanks. You know, the who, what, where, when, how"—I roll my eyes—"and why you haven't been in his life since, in ever so long."

Ondine pouts. "I'd rather not. I mean, I feel as if I'd be speaking out of school." She nods towards Jack. "I don't want Teacher to give me a demerit—or even worse, a spanking." She bats her lashes. "Then again, it wouldn't be the first time."

Seriously? She wants to go *there*—with *Jack's wife?*

I'll also be serving her dinner within the hour, and I've been known to add a little non-detectable somethin'-somethin' to an impudent guest's food that causes a quick heart attack.

Thus far, with her, it hasn't come to that. Still, I'm sure she'll appreciate a fair warning: "Jack and I are adults. We had lives before meeting each other. Like most couples, we've had our ups and downs. But we're together—eight years and counting—because we love and trust each other. So, if you're trying to make me jealous, don't bother. It won't work."

"Now, why would I do that?" Ondine purrs. "I love him too—and deeply. I always will. He gets it. Maybe it's because he's the one man who knows me better than I know myself. Or maybe it's because I know he'll always love me too." She smiles supremely. "Go ahead. Ask him." But then she thinks a moment, and adds, "Ah! Perhaps that's why he's never mentioned me. No matter. I just wanted you to have the lay of the land. And now that Lee has agreed to my proposal for the documentary, you—and Jack—will be seeing a lot of me."

"Doubtful," I huff. "There is no love lost between Jack and Lee. If anything, it's even more reason for him to stay away."

As soon as the words leave my mouth, I could bite my

tongue. Ondine's smirk proves I've played a card I may later regret.

---

## SCINTILLATING CONVERSATION? *NOT.*

Or maybe the animated dinner-table chatter of your guests just feels that way when you're a bit tipsy.

Or maybe it's because your husband's ex-lover has had him to herself at the other end of the table for the past half hour, and you're too far away to hear their discussion.

Every now and again, her hand will slip under the table. When it does, Jack flinches. I can guess why. I'm sure she's reminding him of all the reasons he should still be with her.

To Jack's credit, he isn't smiling. Not only that, immediately he turns his whole body toward the nearest guest on his other side—Trisha—who is still chuffed with pride at how well-timed our gathering has been thus far, and rightly so. Now free to gossip with Jeff and Janie, she doesn't give Jack anything more than a quick hand squeeze or nod—

Leaving him alone to fend off Ondine's less-than-gentle touches and whispered asides.

On my right is Lee, and James is on my left. Aunt Phyllis is on James's other side. She's got Porter beside her, and Jody is next to him. Of course, Dominic is on Jody's other side, and Teddy on his. Abu is on the other side of Teddy.

The seat between Teddy and Ondine is vacant. Suddenly, I remember who's missing:

*Cheever.*

I should worry, but now he's the least of my problems.

Ondine finds a reason to wave at me. Though I want to ignore her, it's impossible when she loudly declares, "Donna! Isn't it exciting? Mary and Evan will be living together off campus!"

*What the…*

*They're doing what?…*

*Without first running it by me?*

I look up to find Mary smiling at me. Evan gives me a thumbs up—

But when they see the hurt in my face, they exchange confused glances.

"I know what you're thinking," Ondine taunts. "In your day, they called it 'living in sin.'" She lifts a brow. "But if you're to be a part of their lives, you've got to let your grown children make their own choices, am I right?"

*In my day?… Why, she's my age or older!*

Okay, maybe a *few* months younger. Not more than… six?…

Okay maybe fourteen…

I look down at my plate because I don't want anyone to see the tears welling up in my eyes.

---

WHILE EVERYONE HAS their fill of food, folks, and fun, I lean into Dominic's sherry—or what's left of it. He's already bogarted one of the bottles. He's upset because Jody and

Teddy are taking turns jabbing the same punching bag: in this case, him.

Would it have been better if Jody had left in a huff or if Teddy had put her in a chokehold? Of course not. But he's too vain to see that.

Taking a page from their book, Jack becomes the target of my snark.

My hits are subtle, but he still glowers. For example, I tease Porter about his driveway spill by saying, "A little white lie is okay. The bigger things—like coy texts from strangers—can break up a marriage."

And then there's my very loud aside to Dominic: "I think it's just super awesome that your girlfriends like each other! But do yourself a favor and don't ever pick between them"—pointedly, I stare at Ondine—"because the minute you do and the other shows up at your doorstep and waltzes right in as if she owns the place, you'll lose one anyway."

Jack's scowl is uncalled for, but Dominic's perplexed horror is expected. It's just dawned on him that I'm the last person to help him lick his wounds.

He's right. He'll have to seek solace elsewhere.

The slings and arrows of my latest blithe-but-oh-too-loud snarl have my children's heads swiveling from one opponent to the other as if they're watching a Wimbledon match: "Most marriages never last 'until death do we part,' especially when the husband is caught red-handed. The only man any wife can count on is her divorce attorney."

In time, Mary pulls me into the kitchen. "Mom, why

were you upset when Ondine mentioned Evan and I had moved in together?"

"Because... because I..." What am I going to tell her, that I ignored the many texts and calls she made to reach me?

From the look on her face, I've just answered her question.

"So, you really didn't know." Mary puts her head on my shoulder. "I'm sorry you had to hear about it from Ondine! I hadn't realized until it was too late that she overheard Evan and I discussing it. And I didn't know she'd blurt it out that way—"

"Forget about it." I kiss her cheek. "To your credit, you attempted to bring it up several times. If things hadn't been so hectic—"

She lifts her head so that we're eye to eye. "Is something going on between you and Dad?"

She already knows the answer to that when I look away.

"Please! Just talk to him. Ask him to be honest with you," Mary insists. "For your relationship. *For all of us.*"

She's right.

ABU AND JACK are in an animated discussion about the latest Lakers game. No better time to take my husband aside and let him know he's off the hook.

For now, anyway.

The jury is still out until he comes clean about Ondine.

I put my hands on his shoulder. Instinctively, he shudders. Is he afraid I'll ring his neck?

To assure him I won't, in a gentle voice, I ask, "Do you mind if I borrow my husband for a moment?"

Abu laughs. "By all means. There's only so much shit you can shoot with someone you see almost every day." His gaze moves to Teddy, on his other side. "I think I can keep myself occupied."

From Teddy's smile, I know he's right. And I've no doubt Abu can make Teddy's defection worth it.

I take Jack's arm and walk him through the kitchen and out the back door.

# 10

# Musical Chairs

*Despite having persevered with a seating map so harmonious that it would make any consulate diplomat jealous, all your hard work goes to naught when your guests take it upon themselves to move around your place cards. And no, you shouldn't excuse them because they didn't know that moving a few cards puts your cousins who do much more than kiss side by side, not to mention those two aunts in a long-held vendetta within spitting distance of each other.*

*But since you can't excuse yourself from greeting late guests to tackle the card-shifting culprits, let alone tether your guests to their seats, there is one thing you can—and should do:*

*Buy a cattle prod. That way, if all else fails and your guests' messy moves are still accomplished, those who misbehave will be shocked—literally—to know you're annoyed and that you won't tolerate it.*

*Then pray they don't like the sensation.*

MY GAME PLAN was to be subtle, but since I'm already slurring words, that ship has sailed. Instead, I blurt out, "Who is she to you?"

Jack's silence speaks volumes:

She's someone whom he once loved.

Someone who hurt him dearly.

More to the point, she is someone he still feels deeply for.

But Jack says none of this. Instead, he stares away because he knows his answer is weak and bogus: "The documentarian... Ondine is ...Well, she's someone from my past."

"Duh. I guessed as much when I saw the look in your eyes when she came in with Lee." By moving closer, I force him to look me in the eye. "And... you still love her."

"Yes... *No*... I mean... Donna...you don't understand. It's complicated." He looks down at his feet. "To top it off, knowing why she's here today is above your pay grade."

"Screw that old chestnut!" Frustrated, I throw up my hands. "How and why you know her has nothing to do with this mission. It's personal."

"You're right! It is personal. But that still doesn't mean I can tell you why she's here."

"Then, enjoy her company. But I don't have to."

I make my way to the playhouse. It's the only place I can think to hide without running into a guest who will rightly see the desolation in my face.

Jack follows and grabs my arm just as I reach its threshold. "You can't just walk away from a houseful of people!"

"Oh, no? Watch me." I fling open the door—

To the biggest shock of my life:

The playhouse's single bed is rumpled. Its desk holds one plate piled high with white turkey meat and another with one of the precious turkey legs and a thigh. A bowl is spooned high with Yukon potatoes swimming in gravy. Another bowl is filled with sweet potato soufflé. There is also half of a cherry pie. Over a long, narrow table, three video monitors have been mounted to the wall. They roam through different parts of the Craig household. Another monitor, sitting directly on the table, is playing a porn movie.

Cheever sits at the desk.

"What the hell is going on here?" Jack roars.

"Calm down, dude! It's all good. Great, in fact. Your Mini Me's, Jeff and Trisha, are paying me to stay out of your hair." Cheever shrugs. "I'm no sucker. If I can make a few bucks doing a disappearing act, why not?" He chuckles. "Hey, maybe this is a great idea for a new subscription service. People can pay me to stay *out of* their lives. Talk about a way to make passive income!"

I tap the monitor that shows the upstairs hallway. "From the looks of things, you're still in our lives—in the worst possible way!"

"I'm just trying out a new social media concept that will have me rolling in dough—especially if my agent can sell it to a streamer! Think of it as a new-school version of Candid

Camera, except harsher and sexier." He nods toward the video monitor in our upstairs hallway. "And you guys are my pitch deck. You've heard of 'WandaVision,' right? Well, this is 'DonnaDrama.' Ta-*dah*!"

He clicks onto another screen, which shows a Power-Point presentation titled:

## DonnaDrama!
## It Makes the Housewives Franchise Seem Like a Monastery!

"This invasion of privacy that can send you back to the hoosegow," I point out.

"Not if you get the owners' permission to allow you to tap into their security cameras and then sweeten the deal by paying them based on their feed's click-through rate and views-per-minute," Cheever counters.

"Well, you didn't. You recorded us without our permission." Jack takes Cheever's computer, takes it to the play-house's sink, turns on the tap, and puts it underwater.

"What the hell, Mr. Craig? I've already got my first subscriber lined up—"

"Oh yeah? And who is that?" I ask.

"The documentarian that Chiffray is boinking—that Ondine chick."

Jack grabs Cheever by the collar. Is he that upset that about Ondine and Lee's relationship?

*My world really is falling apart!*

"Stay here until I come to get you. Or else," Jack snarls.

Cheever nods. He knows better than to say anything, let alone argue. Maybe because Jack is choking him.

The only reason Jack loosens his grip is to answer his buzzing cell phone. By his look, I instantly know that whatever he says won't make me happy.

Sharply, I ask, "What's wrong now?... No, let me guess. Some third woman has shown up claiming to be Dominic's plus one."

Jack winces. "Even worse. Ryan is on his way."

"What? *HERE?*... and NOW?"

He shows me his phone, which has a text sent under the covert name that Jack has assigned to Ryan.

## TheDevilWearsBrooksBrothers
## COMING OVER

"Ah, great! Just great! What's happened now, another deepfake?"

Jack shrugs. "Seriously, I couldn't tell you."

"No matter. What difference does it make? He'll have something to rant and rave over the minute he gets here." I try to shake off my anger, but I can't.

"If you're worried about our guests, they work with him too and are used to it, so his ranting won't make any difference to them," Jack points out.

"Our children don't work for Acme. And the last thing I need today is to have them see us grovel in front of our boss. What kind of example will that set?"

Jack snorts. "It may be the nail on the coffin for any

inkling they have to enter the field of diplomatic intelligence."

"Oh... Right! You've got a point there. If having dodged bullets and bombs and terrorists and the occasional kidnapping hasn't already turned them off to our profession, hearing us getting yelled at for no reason may be exactly what they need to see." My sarcasm doesn't even raise an eyebrow. "I guess we can do nothing at this point except set one more place at the table."

There's another ping on Jack's cell. He stares down. "Um...make that two. He's bringing someone—and he's at the door right now!" Jack's cackle is mirthless. "If only Ryan and his plus one had gotten here at the same time as Lee and his, this nightmare might have ended by now."

"What do you mean by that?"

For some reason, he hesitates before answering. In time, he says, "Let's just say that the sooner everyone gets here, stuffs their bellies, and leaves, the better."

We go back inside. As we make our way to the front door, I peek through the living room window. The woman with Ryan is a pretty blonde. Whatever he's saying now puts a sweet smile on her face. The way he's grinning, it's obvious they've been friends for some time. Quite frankly, I'm relieved he's with someone who can keep his mind off the deepfake and terrorist dramas, if only for the day.

I fling open the door. "So glad you could make it, Ryan!"

He nods toward his date. "This is an old friend, Carol Wise. Because of the travel embargo, she's stranded here.

And since you're the most gracious hostess and the best home chef I know—"

"Today's motto is 'the more, the merrier.'" I hold out my hand, adding, "Any friend of Ryan's is a friend of ours."

Carol nods her thanks. "The feeling is mutual. Ryan says so many wonderful things about you that I can tell he sees you as family."

"Ah!... Well, I feel the same way." I can't keep the quiver out of my voice.

Ryan must hear it, too, because he leans in to kiss me on the cheek—

But then he pulls back.

As Carol goes in, he mutters, "Try to stay sober. Today, of all days, I need you firing on all cylinders."

*What the hell does that mean?*

Maybe it's good that they'll be sitting at the other end of the table.

Still, I rinse my mouth before returning to the dining room.

# 11

# Breast, Leg, Thigh, or Wing?

*Ah, the dilemma every hostess faces when doling out the tasty bits of her main Thanksgiving course! Each bird offers only two legs, two thighs, and two wings. Even the breast of the largest bird is never near enough for your ravenous diners, let alone for the leftovers craved by your dear family. My oh my! What's a chef-hostess to do?*

*Should the victors be the basis of first come, first served?*

*Heaven forfend that the one who shouts it loudest is rewarded for their rude entreaty!*

*Arm-wrestling wouldn't be fair. What if your fragile grandmother draws the short straw against her brawniest grandson?*

*Here's a thought: initiate tournament bouts of Rock-Paper-Scissors until every part of the bird is dissected. It's a much better solution than a forty-pace pistol duel among the contestants. Think of the ammo you'll save—*

*Not to mention, there will be no bodies to bury!*

BY THE TIME I return to the dining room, Ryan has taken Carol to the table's only open seat: beside Ondine, who is listening intently while Mary gushes about something. Evan is also hanging on her every word. In the meantime, Jeff finds another chair for Ryan. Though I would have assumed Ryan would have also sat next to Ondine, he places his chair on the other side of Carol, between her and Jack.

"That end of the table filled up after all," James points out.

I shrug. "You can never have too much of a good thing, right?"

"Old friends?" he asks.

"A friend, yes. But Ryan is also my boss. Carol is his friend."

James glances around the table. "This is so... *normal*."

"What do you usually do on Thanksgiving?"

He chuckles. "We're always on the move, so I'm rarely stateside for the holidays."

"Surely you still have family here," I counter.

"I do, yes. But... I rarely see them."

"Why not?"

"My children are grown. One can be anywhere in the world at any given point in time. Unfortunately, my child with a family doesn't speak to me." James's eyes roam down the length of the table. When they come to the children, they stop. There, Jeff is laughing at Trisha and Janie's antics. At the same time, Mary buries herself in Evan's arms.

"My mother died when I was only thirteen," I explain. "Cancer. Not a day goes by that I don't miss her. I inherited her love of holidays. After she died, my father drank himself to death. He got to walk me down the aisle with my first husband but never met my children. I know he would have loved to have done so." I pat James's hand. "Trust me when I say it's never too late to make amends."

"Sometimes... well, sometimes the punishment fits the crime." For once, he meets my gaze with those bottle-green eyes...

So much like Jack's.

And those cheekbones. Like Jack's, too.

And the tiny bend in his nose.

*My God...*

He's not James Gregg, but James Craig Sr.

*He is Jack's father.*

At that moment, I remember the texts and the note Ondine left for Jack:

***I know you asked me never to contact you, but I love and miss you...***

And:

***Please, Jack! Our chance encounter made me realize I love you too much to walk away forever. Can I see you?...***

I murmur, "You're Jack's father, aren't you? And Ondine is his sister."

James nods.

"She reached out to him," I admit. "She misses him terribly."

Once again, I hear the cadence of Jack's laugh coming from James. But he's shaking his head. "She would have never done that."

"But... I saw the texts myself! And I read a note she sent—"

"Ah!...So... you saw those?" He thinks for a moment. Finally he comes out with it: "If you're talking about the missives from O.M., let me assure you. Those were from me."

"*You?*... but those are her initials—O.M."

"I'm sorry you were confused. You see, Jack has always called her Dina, which is short for 'Ondine.' I was the one who reached out to him—by the nickname he always called me when he still cared about me: 'Old Man.'"

"Why didn't he want to meet with you?"

"Because..." He looks away, as if seeking the right words to make his point. "Donna, like your former husband, Carl, I'm a traitor to this country. I'm a Russian operative, as is Ondine." James takes a deep breath. "It doesn't surprise me that Jack never shared this with you. It is his biggest shame. It was his mother's, too. When she found out, she committed suicide. Her death haunts me to this day."

*Jack's father and sister are Russian spies?...*

No wonder he's never talked about his family.

"Initially, we came for the brush pass with Barry Telford, and to embed and then activate the trojan that made your country's commercial airlines a fleet of death machines," James explains.

It was James who made the brush pass to Barry. No wonder he looked so familiar to me.

And it was Ondine who accosted Jack when he tried to stop it.

"But then the opportunity to meet with Lee presented itself, which enlarged our mission," James continues. "Considering his diplomatic connections, working on his documentary puts us in the catbird seat for even more subterfuge—at the expense of Lee's reputation, which, if Ondine has her way, may turn him from an unknowing asset into an unwilling one—but a Russian asset nonetheless." James sighs deeply. "Little did I know it would also put me down the street from my son, you, and my wonderful grandchildren."

"And now you and Dina are stranded here."

"An ironic twist of fate, isn't it?" Realizing I'm stunned by the news, he sighs.

I try hard to keep my voice from trembling when I ask, "James, why have you told me this?"

He looks down at his plate. "I think you know why."

"Because you have the SD card with the passcode that can disconnect the Trojan with you now," I murmur.

"I did, but I've left it here—with you." James bows his head. We sit in silence. In time, he says, "Donna, you have given me the greatest gift: the chance to see my son's happiness. He has a wife and a family who cherish him. In honor of his success in accomplishing something I never could—

stability and an honorable life—I've left it with you. It's in your closet, in the pocket of that Hello Kitty purse." His eyes are glazed with tears. "It once belonged to Mary, didn't it?"

"Yes. Aunt Phyllis gave it to her when she was six, maybe seven. Mary took it everywhere. When she became a teen, she tossed it. I pulled it out of the trash because I couldn't let it go."

With a melancholy smile, James gazes out at our family and guests. "This has been the best day of my life. But it's time I take my leave before Ondine discovers what I've done."

"I'll make sure she doesn't," I vow.

"Fair warning, Donna; it may come down to you—or her."

Despite being his sister, Jack would never choose a Russian operative over his country-

Or over me.

*I must believe that.*

James grasps my hand tightly and then rises from the table. I know he's slipped out of the house when I see him go past the window. He's heading up the hill to Lion's Lair.

I feel a tap on my shoulder. "I say, old girl, Isn't it time to break out the desserts?" Dominic sounds desperate to move the party along. And no wonder. Both Jody and Teddy are now flirting with Abu.

"Great idea." In a voice loud enough to get everyone's attention, I announce, "Thanks for bringing your plates into the kitchen. Desserts are laid out on the kitchen table, along with coffees and teas."

Not everyone gets up at once. Carol is in deep discussion with Ondine, who, I presume, is feeding her some bullshit about the documentary that will never happen.

While joining the others moving toward the kitchen, I suddenly feel ravenous. It dawns on me that I haven't eaten a bite of food.

I go back into the kitchen. While I cut a piece of pecan pie for myself, I glance around. Everyone is talking and laughing. They are enjoying themselves. For the first time, I can do that too.

I wonder how Lee will react when he hears that he's hosting the Russian spies who are terrorizing the country? He'll feel much better if I couple it with the news that I now have the SD card. In the meantime, Acme can detain Ondine until the FBI arrives.

There's no better time than now to let Ryan in on her little secret.

The others, pie plates in hand, are also trickling into the dining room. But when I look around, Ondine is nowhere to be found.

I try my best to keep the anxiety out of my voice as I ask, "Has anyone seen Ondine?"

"Since the hall powder room was occupied, she went upstairs," Mary offers.

*Ah hell.*

I don't run until I reach the hall, and then fly up the staircase.

# 12

# How to Get Rid of Unwanted Guests

*Not everyone who shows up for your most important holiday meal is expected—or wanted, for that matter. But being the hostess, it's best to smile and be gracious, right?*

*Not necessarily.*

*Sure, the smile is crucial—if only to cover up your distaste for the interlopers' uncouth behavior. As for any graciousness, there are subtle ways to drive home the point that next time they should wait for an invitation, or at least beg for one. But now that they're here, you must take matters into your own hands. For example:*

1. *Feel free to seat them far from those whose conversation you find more scintillating. Perhaps the kiddie table? If even that's too close, try another room altogether. Even your back porch will do. If it's blustery outside, all the better!*

2. *Make sure their portions are smaller than everyone else's. And, if they ask for seconds, tell them you've got nothing to spare. Sure, it's a blatant lie, but who cares? You counted on leftovers to feed your family for a few extra days... Okay, maybe throw the uninvited a bone—and hope they choke on it.*

3. *Don't serve your good wines to these unwanted guests—especially since you plan to spike their glasses with something that makes them pass out. When they do, put them to bed—permanently. That is, six feet under. Nothing is too drastic for party crashers. And you know what they say: out of sight, out of mind!*

———

I'VE NEVER RUN upstairs so fast, but I slow down when I get to the grandfather clock at the head of the hall. I need the element of surprise, especially if Ondine has a weapon. Even if she didn't bring one, I've got two hidden in the bedroom. The last thing I need is to be shot with my own gun. But I've also got one hidden in the grandfather clock. I take it out.

In a few silent strides, I'm at the master bedroom door. I glance around. Nothing looks out of order—

But then something does: my closet door is opened just slightly.

I run into it. Is the SD card where James said he left it— in Trisha's old Hello Kitty purse?

Yes! Thank goodness!

Immediately, I see that Ondine was here because she left a Polaroid photo taped to my closet's full-length mirror.

In it, Ondine holds Nicky in her arms. Smiling supremely, she stares straight into the camera. She's written something on back of the photo:

**I took my little date to Slippery Slope!
DROP EVERYTHING, OR I DROP HIM.
AND BRING <u>IT</u> WITH YOU.**

Slippery Slope is the sheerest side of Lion's Lair. The drop is fifteen hundred feet into the ocean.

It feels as though time has stopped. Below me, in the living room, I hear Emma laughing with Trisha and Janie as they clear the table. Arnie is with Jeff in his bedroom. They've snuck off to continue their ongoing game of League of Legends.

Each of Nicky's parents assumes the other has eyes and ears on him.

I can't let them know how close he is to danger.

Not now.

Not when every second counts.

I'm out the door in a flash.

THE WIND CARRIES Nicky's cries.

I follow it up the hill crowned by a bramble patch. Its other side is a steep drop into the Pacific Ocean.

When I crest the hill, I see them next to the cliff. Although she holds him tight, he struggles. He's wearing a harness that is on a very long bungee tether.

But what is it tied to, if anything at all?

When she spots me, Ondine waves me over.

It takes twenty strides to put me within ten feet of them. Seeing me, Nicky's tears stop. Desperately, he reaches out for me. "Donna, I don't like her! She swung me too high in the air!"

Despite the wind, Ondine's cruel laugh sends chills through me. "My God, I was just practicing!" She shrugs. "Can I help it if the little brat is a scaredy cat?"

"You truly are a sick bitch!" I retort.

Ondine clucks her tongue. "Such a potty mouth! Donna, you are truly a lousy influence on children."

I retort, "Says someone who is terrorizing a child!"

Lifting him high, Ondine growls, "Don't tempt me."

I hold up the SD card. "Cut the theatrics. Just put Nicky down."

The card's purple and green marks show her that it's the real deal. "Drop it over there—on that stump." Ondine points to something behind me.

I turn around. I don't see it. "Where? What stump?"

"What—are you blind? Over there—by the south side of the cliff."

I scan the hilltop. Then I see it, at least a hundred yards

off. If I drop it there, Ondine will leave Nicky while she retrieves it. I'll have to grab him first so that he's safe. But by the time I do, she'll be long gone.

As if reading my mind, she chuckles. "I know what you're thinking. My God, what kind of friend would you be if you put your country before the safety of Emma's child?"

Hearing her, Nicky kicks harder and screams louder, shouting for me.

Of course, I have no choice. I run to the stump and lay the card on top of it.

By now, she's dropped Nicky on the ground and strides toward the stump. He runs toward me, too, but he can only go so far before his tether jerks him back.

I shout over the wind, "Don't worry, Nicky! Stay perfectly still—like a statue! I'll be right there."

I'm halfway to Nicky when she passes me. My spittle spatters her face.

Angrily, she wipes it away. "Stupid, stupid, Donna! You should have never done that. Now I'm going to have to shoot him"—she pulls out a Glock—"or you, which means he dies anyway."

Seeing the gun, Nicky cries even louder.

I freeze.

In time, Ondine mutters, "That's better." She keeps moving toward her prize.

I run to Nicky. When he sees this, he runs toward me too—

Only to be snapped back by the bungee cord—

Which flings him over the cliff.

When I reach the spike that tethers him to the cord, I drop to my knees and then I pull him up, all the while talking sweetly, calmly, explaining that he has no reason to cry because I'm here and I'll pull him to my side, and we'll go home together, where he can have as much pie as he wants. This calms him down enough that I can finally look at the stump.

The SD card is gone, and so is Ondine.

With Nicky in hand, I walk down the hill and to my car as quickly as possible. "Sweetie, reach into my pocket and grab my cell."

His eyes grow wide. His parents won't let him play with theirs.

When he has it in his hand, I unlock it and then hand it back. "Hit the number seven."

He does as I ask. It's Emma's speed dial number.

Emma answers. "Donna? I can't find Nicky anywhere—"

Hearing her voice, Nicky declares, "I'm right here, Mommy! I'm with Donna! The bad lady took me up the scary hill!"

Emma is incoherent, laughing and crying at the same time, sputtering about what an awful mother she is for letting her little guy out of her sight, even for just a few minutes, and what a great friend I am, and how she'll always be indebted to me, that she loves me like a sister.

And then she says, "Where was he?"

All I have to say is, "Ondine has the SD card. She took him...as leverage." Emma knows now what I know.

After a long silence, she says softly but deadly, "Let's take her down."

It's the answer I'd expect from any mother. "On it."

I can't help but laugh as I run the rest of the way. Nicky, relieved, giggles.

If only he knew.

Maybe when he's older—an adult—I'll tell him about his role in saving the world.

If I'm still alive.

If the world is still around.

---

I'VE JUST WALKED onto the veranda when I hear a big explosion.

It comes from Lion's Lair.

Every home in Hilldale opens its door as our neighbors run out to see what has happened.

Our front door also opens as my guests run to the street.

Seeing me with Nicky, Emma, Arnie, Lee, and Jack run over to me. Nicky reaches out to his parents, who grab him in a bear hug.

Just like my family does with me.

Jack nods at Lee, who stands to one side. "I think it's time we tell Donna what's been happening. Don't you?"

Lee sighs, relieved. "Hell, yeah! I thought you'd never

ask." He glances around. "But it's a conversation we should have at Lion's Lair."

He nods to Porter.

In no time, Lee's security team is driving Jack, Lee, Ryan, Carol, and me up the hill in one car, and our children in another. Our Acme team is right behind them.

# 13

# How to Avoid Boring Dinner Conversations

*It's easy to assume that those who grace your Thanksgiving table will walk over your threshold with smiles on their faces, joy in their hearts, and all the right things flowing from their mouths.*

*WRONG.*

*Plan on your guests being just as stressed as you are—*

*Albeit with hardly any legitimate reason to be so. I mean, let's face it: all on your lonesome, you've made the meal and provided the incredible setting in which they will enjoy it.*

*So, what right do they have to rain on your parade?*

*They don't.*

*And here's what you do to make sure it won't happen:*

*First, sit the complainers together and far away. That way, any and all kvetching reaches the ears of those who can appreciate it and not the ones who won't. (By that, I mean YOU.)*

*Next, put a sleeping powder in their drinks. Better they should snore than grouse in public.*

*Finally, consider hiring a fact-checker. Give this person a buzzer that can be pushed whenever a guest lets loose with a whopper—*

*Except if it's to compliment the hostess on providing a divine meal.*

---

THE ADULTS HAVE MOVED into Lee's study. Porter, always the sentry, closes the door behind us.

"Okay, who wants to start?" My gaze shifts from Jack to Lee and then to Ryan. Eve is here, too. But after serving coffee, she sits beside Lee—

Who takes her hand and kisses it.

For the first time, Eve wears an engagement ring.

*Well, it's about damn time.*

Ryan's harumph gets my attention. "How much did James tell you?" he asks.

"Apparently, not nearly enough," I reply. "I mean, yeah, okay, he divulged that he and Ondine were FSB operatives. And that they were responsible for the terrorism that brought all flights to a halt. And that they paid Barry Telford to embed the cellular microchips with the malware too turn them into nano bombs. But apparently, James left out another of their great deeds. Like, why the hell did they blow up Lion's Lair too?"

"It's only one cottage on the property, not all of the estate," Jack points out.

"And it's because they'd hoped to assassinate Libby Kentfield," Lee admits.

I'm so stunned at this revelation that I flop onto a chair. "My God! Is Libby here too? ... And is she..."

"Not to worry, Donna. Libby is fine," Lee assures me. "She is at Lion's Lair, and she did walk into one of its cottages, but that was to mislead Ondine and James. It's not public knowledge, but like the main house, all the cottages have safe rooms. They are also connected to the main house via bomb-proof underground tunnels. In truth, Libby has been secured in one of the mansion's suites with no outside windows."

"Why is Libby here, especially during this terrorist crisis?" I ask.

"Frankly, she wasn't expected, which is why we had to play hide-and-seek with her accommodations," Lee continues. "She was to spend Thanksgiving with her siblings and their children at her sister's home in San Diego. But when the airline and cellular embargoes took effect, she had Air Force One detour to Andrews Air Force Base. From there, her motorcade brought her here."

I'm still confused. "Why come here at all? Why not just fly back to the White House?"

"As the new executive director of the NCC—the NSA's National Counterterrorism Center, Carol can best answer that," Ryan replies.

So, Carol isn't just a pretty face who caught Ryan's fancy? Well, surprise, surprise!

"With the seven-day flight and communications embargoes, POTUS's security team felt it would be safer if she stayed away from the White House," Carol explains. "This allowed the NCC to conduct a complete malware analysis of the building's WPS, which, surprisingly, also revealed the White House as Ground Zero for the social media posts feeding a false narrative about a 'deep state.'"

"But couldn't the deepfake have been created anywhere before being uploaded on social media?" I ask.

"Yes—but it wasn't," Carol replies. "For the past few months, several have been coming directly from the White House. The deepfake of Libby at the podium is the most recent example. For some time now, the NCC has been suspicious that Russian Social Design Agency—Russia's intelligence division that creates its social media disinformation—released a trojan in the software running the White House security cameras. This allowed it to collect footage of various rooms and hallways to be used for deepfakes. The malware also transmitted the deepfakes to the White House's WPS."

"How did you discover this?" I ask.

"After the deepfakes began, my team realized that the locations used were not on the public tour," Carol divulges. "Two people who looked suspiciously like Ondine and James were given a private tour a couple of weeks before the deepfakes began, courtesy of a White House Administration official who, for some time, has been suspected of being a Russian asset."

"Let me guess I reply. "This person was part of a

supposed fact-finding junket to Moscow and woke up in the wrong bed without remembering how he got there."

"You nailed it." Carol rolls her eyes.

"Regarding this deepfake latest incident, the NCC traced the upload to Lion's Lair," Ryan replies, "which is how we knew it was Ondine and James."

"Could Ondine and James have been paid by the opposing political party?" I ask.

"In this particular case, Russia was up to its usual shenanigans. And since it would benefit from having the opposing party in the White House, the deepfake couldn't come at a better time to sabotage Libby's second presidential term. Of those politicians thinking of throwing their hats in the ring, there are at least two congresspersons and one senator whose fact-finding boondoggle to Russia included disappearing acts. But that's a discussion for another day." Carol shrugs. "The best part was being at your Thanksgiving dinner to watch the sting go down. I'm so glad I convinced Ryan to barge in—with me as his plus-one, of course. I'm just lucky I made it out of D.C. before the travel and cellular embargoes went into effect!" When she winks at our boss, he laughs. "It also allowed me to test Acme's smart contact lenses." Coyly, she bats her eyes. "I've got to admit, they live up to all the hype I've heard all these years. To top it off, they're quite comfortable! I will suggest to DARPA that it negotiate a license for it."

I ask Carol, "How did you know Ondine and James would be at Lion's Lair in the first place?"

"It was Jack's idea," Carol explains. "He suggested that

we dangle something they couldn't refuse: an invitation from former President Lee Chiffray to discuss a documentary about his charities. Jack knew being close to an ex-president would be catnip for Ondine since Libby was a regular visitor to Lion's Lair."

My gaze moves from Jack to Lee and back again. Frankly, the way they're grinning at each other, I wouldn't be surprised if they suddenly high-fived or chest-bumped.

I guess that's better than being at each other's throats.

"Ondine and James rightly deduced that Lee's cellular system is a WPS well equipped with the necessary security for POTUS's visits," Carol continues. "Their goal was to manually plant a trojan on the WPS as well as transmission malware on Lee's secure cell phone. Knowing this, if they had carried it out anyway, the CIA would have re-routed the WPS to a fake feed, which would have provided a steady stream of misinformation."

"As it turns out, Libby's unscheduled stop gave Ondine the ideal opportunity for the most significant act of terrorism on U.S. soil in over twenty years: the assassination of a sitting American president," Ryan adds.

I turn to Jack. "Did you rendezvous with James on your morning runs?"

He nods. "When he reached out, I played along. I knew he was dying to meet you and the kids, but I didn't agree to letting him until he assured me Ondine would come along too."

"And when she did, you acted shocked and upset," I reply.

"I knew she'd expect that reaction," Jack explains. "If I'd acted otherwise, Ondine would have been suspicious. She knows how ashamed I am at her and my father's treason."

Awed, I declare, "You deserve an Academy Award. You certainly fooled me!"

Jack laughs. "I'm glad I pulled it off."

"From Jack's time in the Air Force to his service with Acme, he has always been upfront about his family with his superiors in the intelligence community," Ryan declares. "Until James came to Hilldale, neither he nor Ondine has ever reached out to him."

"Ondine knew better," Jack mutters. "I would have arranged an FBI sting."

"But Jack, you must have known your father would eventually reach out," I insist. It still haunts me how desperate my ex-husband, Carl, was to insinuate himself in the lives of our children even after his treason was discovered.

"Surprisingly, I never expected it of my father." Jack looks away. "I guess he'd gotten sentimental in his old age."

"Thank goodness for that," I point out. "Otherwise, he wouldn't have left us the SD card containing the passcode that ends the travel and cellular embargoes."

"Only to have Ondine blackmail you with Nicky's life and retake it," Emma retorts.

"Now, if only we could get it back—as well as access the account that holds Acme's fee," Ryan grouses.

Carol looks down at her watch. "Maybe you can make

up some of your losses with your poker winnings. Didn't you say that your annual Thanksgiving game goes all night?"

Ryan perks up. "You bet. And you're more than welcome to join me."

She chuckles. "I thought you'd never ask."

My family and the rest of my dinner party walk out with them. The thought of the mess facing me at home is my biggest incentive to putting this day behind me—

Well, that, and knowing Jack hates Ondine as much as me.

---

FOR AFTER-THANKSGIVING CLEAN-UP, it's all hands on deck. Evan and Jeff clear the table while Trisha and Mary put the leftovers into containers and Jack loads the dishwasher.

Just as I scrape the last plate of its leavings, Jeff taps my shoulder. Noting his anxious frown, I ask, "Honey, what's wrong?"

"Mom, I'm so sorry! Until now, I'd forgotten that Granddad James gave me this! He said he trusted me to give it to you and Dad at the right time—but I may have blown it!" Jeff places something in my hand. It's a shred of paper that reads:

SPYNGER ID: **4028043920 – PW: 0MLuv$U**

. . .

IT'S the code for a GPS tracker. James must have somehow secured it to Ondine.

Jack looks over my shoulder. After reading it, he takes a photo of it and heads out the door.

Confused, Jeff asks, "Where's Dad going?"

"To find them." I also access the GPS's readout on my cell. They are moving toward Beverly Hills. "Jeff, stay here with Mary, Evan, Trisha, and Aunt Phyllis."

My son's eyes grow wide. "Where are you going?"

"To help your father."

Jeff shakes his head. "I hope James is okay."

"Why wouldn't he be?"

"When Ondine drove off, he was lying down in the backseat. He waved, but he didn't look so well."

If Ondine won't hesitate to hurt her father, then Jack is in danger too.

I grab my coat and purse and run out the door.

# 14

# Kitchen Fires

*Big surprise: the kitchen is where most home fires begin: forty-four percent, in fact, of the most recent statistics on fires in the United States, which is over 178,600 incidents. The cause:*

*Seven percent of the time, someone had unintentionally turned on the stove or forgotten to turn it off. Talk about a big oopsie!*

*Another nine percent fail to clean their stoves. Solution: using a little soap and water on a cloth or sponge will cut through your turkey's greasy drippings on the bottom of your oven and around your stove's burners.*

*Another twenty-eight percent walked away from their stoves, more than likely to answer a phone or open the door for their guests. Solution: sure, it's hard to be a great hostess while cooking, so shoo everyone from the kitchen and delegate the chore of providing scintillating conversation to those who can keep your guests entertained while you tend to the meal.*

*Then there are the 10% who leave a combustible near the heat source.*

*Solution: don't store cooking oils, grease, fat, or butter near your Wolf Range.*

*(Tip: the same goes for your bullets and bombs.)*

---

THE BEYOND HEAVENLY FUNERAL HOME is old and grand enough to front two sides of its Los Angeles block. Like me, Jack would know better than to park in the lot, let alone within a two-block distance. My guess? He's slipped in through one of its back doors, so I'll do the same.

Ondine emerges from a limo. It is bachelorette-party-sized, although she's the only one in it. The spy app traced each step:

She ordered it after hustling James into the Ritz Carlton, where, I assume, she watched the life go out of him. She then called a coroner to verify it was a heart attack. And then she ordered a hearse from Beyond Heavenly to come and get the body.

As for the oversized limo? Easy. Why spare any expense, especially when trying to impress a funeral director hungry to sell you the best and most expensive for your dearly departed's journey into the Afterlife?

While he waits, her limo driver vapes outside the car.

I drive two blocks beyond this single-story building designed like a hacienda. After parking the car, I walk back to its entrance.

The front door opens into an well-appointed lobby. It's empty, but there is a reception desk with a bell. A video screen is behind the desk. A montage of cameras feeds into it. To a background of classical music, the screen flashes onto other rooms in the facility: a memorial chapel, a casket showroom, the cremation room, and the hall running between all of this.

The casket showroom is empty. In the chapel, a minister leads a teary congregation.

Jack is sitting in the back row by himself.

In the cremation room, a man with a white rose pinned to the lapel of his jacket—the funeral director, I suppose—greets a tall, elegant woman: Ondine, in dark glasses and a gray-haired wig. She holds a bouquet of roses in her hands.

The man demonstrates how to use the large furnace in front of them: a cremator. I watch as he points toward a beautiful white closed casket:

James's, I assume.

It sits on rails that lead into an open chamber of a furnace. To one side of the opening are three buttons. As he describes each function, she nods and wipes away a tear. Finally, he does a half-bow and leaves the room.

I take that moment to ring the bell twice.

The funeral director straightens his back and pats the rose in his lapel before heading my way.

By the time he gets to the desk, my face reflects the proper amount of turmoil. I hold out my hand. "Hello, my name is Linda Smith. I'm preparing for the inevitable demise of a terminally ill patient. Would you mind explaining your establishment's various packages for a tradi-tional funeral?"

"But of course! My name is Frank Causey." He motions for me to take one of the two chairs facing the desk.

While he opens a drawer to pull out a brochure, I look up at the screen in time to see Jack slipping out of the chapel. I watch as he heads to his next destination: the crematorium.

At the same time, Ondine takes something out of James's kerchief pocket and puts it in her purse. Mission accomplished, she pushes one of the cremator's buttons.

Ondine waits for the cremator to reach the optimum temperature for incineration. She has her back to the door. The machine must hum loudly enough that she doesn't hear Jack enter.

I nod sagely as Frank explains my coffin choices. I make him elaborate on his most expensive model. As he points out a particular feature, I push the button that freezes the video scroll to one camera: that of the crematorium.

Ondine doesn't realize Jack is behind her.

Between sobs, I ask questions that divert Frank's atten-tion from what I now see: Jack has got Ondine in a choke-hold. Still, her strength is formidable, and her defensive moves are impressive.

As Frank launches into a pitch for a premium ground funeral, I ask that he go into detail about the cemetery's plots with the best views of downtown Los Angeles. While he rummages through the desk for a photo album, I look up at the screen in time to see Ondine kick Jack hard enough for him to grimace and flinch from his pain.

Still, Ondine is no match for him. When he breaks her neck, she goes limp like a rag doll.

As Frank points to a photo of Beyond Heavenly's newest crypt, Jack drops Ondine's body to the floor so that he can open the casket. When he picks her up again, it's to shove her on top of James, face down.

Old Man would have loved knowing he went into a fiery Afterlife with her.

I'm asking Frank whether any celebrities are buried in Beyond Heavenly when, with a push of the button, Ondine and James's casket rides the rails leading into the cremator.

But Jack doesn't notice that Ondine's purse is also on the conveyor belt. By the time he does, it's gone into the cremator.

Realizing the SD card is a goner, Jack slams his hand against the wall, cursing. He's loud enough he's heard over the video's background music.

There's no better time than now for me to wail about my fear of death. It's enough of a distraction that Frank turns from the monitor to me.

I keep up the sob fest until the cremator's light indicates Ondine and James are turned to ash. I wait until Jack reaches the lobby before calming down enough to vow, "I'm living forever."

Frank sighs longingly. "Wishful thinking. But I get it: the choices are overwhelming. Still, you'll rest easy the sooner you make them."

I thank Frank for his time—and for the complimentary hanky that comes with his brochures.

Always the gentleman, Jack holds the door open so that I may walk out first.

---

"YOU SHOULDN'T HAVE FOLLOWED ME." Jack's annoyance shows itself in his growl.

I roll my eyes. "Oh yeah! Like, shame on me for crashing your hit!"

"You're a witness to it, and it's unsanctioned," he reminds me.

"A wife can't testify against her husband," I remind him. "And in this case, I'm pretty sure that President Kentfield would gladly pardon you. In fact, I'm sure she'll give you a medal for saving her life."

Jack shrugs. "Ryan won't be happy that I didn't secure the SD card."

"He'll have to live with the fact that, while the SD card may have gone up in smoke, at least Acme's retainer may still be traceable," I point out.

"I wouldn't blame the Germans for not paying up," he counters.

"Then again, they wouldn't want exposure for how it went down, so maybe the BND will bury its participation in this fiasco with a big fat fee for Acme," I argue.

Jack shows his appreciation for my perspective with a long, lush kiss. When we part, he murmurs, "You always put things into perspective. I knew I married you for a good reason."

"When we get home, I'll remind you of a few more. If you break a speed record, we may even need another shower."

We make it home in record time.

# 15

# Wishbone

*The one way Thanksgiving invites great luck is by breaking the turkey's wishbone. Or, in medical terminology, the "furcula."*

*It takes two to tackle this task. Each contender grabs an end—the clavicle—and pulls hard until it breaks. The one who holds the largest piece gets their wish granted—which, by design, will include the bone's centerpiece, also known as the "interclavicle."*

*On rare occasions, both contenders get their wish honored—*

*But only if they've wished for the same thing.*

*Handy tip: make a wish with someone who knows what you want and wants it too.*

THE TABLE IS CLEARED, and the kitchen is as clean as a whistle.

That's the upside of having children who appreciate what you do for them and our country. I don't have to face a mountain of dishes too.

I open the fridge to find it lined with the goodie bags that Evan and Mary will take back with them to Berkeley. Not surprisingly, it includes generous portions of all four pies.

Trisha and Jeff are on the couch. Mary sits on Evan's lap in the Barcalounger. The kids are watching a classic: *Addams Family Values*. But when Mary beckons us over, Jeff turns off the television.

"Is James okay?" The worry in his tone is palpable.

Jack nods. "We assume he's long gone. So in that regard, all's well that ends well for him... and for us." His lie is smooth enough that even I believe him.

Because Mary's eyes shift to me, I do my best to keep a smile on my lips. To her, Jack's moods are enigmas. She's always been able to read me better.

Mary rises and puts her arm around him. Her relieved nod proves she's bought into Jack's fib.

Holding her tight, Jack murmurs, "So, when will you and Evan return to Berkeley?"

"We'll drive back on Saturday. You know, to beat the I-5 gridlock—which will be even worse, what with the travel and cellular embargoes." Hesitantly, she asks, "Mom, will it be over anytime soon?"

I shake my head. "I wish I could give you an answer. But honey, I can't. Not now, anyway—"

"Dad...Mom! Look at this!" Trisha's voice comes from the dining room.

We find her standing beside the china cabinet. A tiny green velvet jewelry box is nestled in one of the teacups.

Jack's eyes grow large. "My mother had one just like it," he murmurs.

I open the cabinet's glass door, but I don't pick up the jewelry box until Jack nods.

A locket sits inside. It is solid gold, and carved with leaves and vines. On its back is an inscription:

### *James to Abby*
### *April 17, 1976*

There is a chill in Jack's voice. "This was supposed to be Ondine's. If she'd known he left it for me, she'd blow her stack."

"Put on the locket, Mom!" Mary insists.

My gaze goes to Jack. "If my wearing your mother's locket makes you uncomfortable, I won't."

"Not at all. I'm just glad the old man never hocked it." Jack shrugs. "Ondine would have done so, if given the chance."

After taking it out, I hand it to Jack, who slips it around my neck.

"It's beautiful!" Mary exclaims.

"One day, it will be yours," I vow.

Mary chuckles. "I'm holding you to that. Of course, Trisha will fight me for it."

Trisha mutters, "You better believe it!"

Ignoring her, Mary nudges Jack. "What do you think, Dad?"

Jack looks heavenward. "Your mother has been unlucky with lockets. You may get it even sooner."

"What's inside?" Mary wonders.

I open the locket. It holds two photos. One is of Ondine's and Jack's mother, Abby. The other is of Abby holding a toddler.

"Dad, is that you?" Mary asks. "Wait...don't answer that! Of course it is."

Jack scrutinizes it. "I've never seen this photo before, but from those jug ears, I guess you're right."

"Beautiful! I'll cherish it always," I whisper. I attempt to close the locket's clasp, but it refuses to click. "Odd..."

"Dad, maybe one of the photos shifted," Mary suggests. "The one of you and your Grandmother Abby."

Jack takes a closer look. "You're right." To reposition it, he lifts it first—

But then he freezes. "There's something under here." Jack looks up, perplexed. "Hey, Donna, hand me a tweezer."

I go to the downstairs powder room, grab one from a drawer, and run back.

When I return, I can tell that Jack hasn't moved. "Gently, now, lift the photo out of the frame."

I follow his instructions—

Which reveals a tiny black dot. "Well, what do you know," Jack murmurs.

"What is it?" Mary asks.

"A microdot," I explain. "Do you think Ondine transferred the intel that Barry Telford had stolen from the SD card to it?"

Jack guffaws. "If so, you're now wearing the passcode to initiate or abort the launch of several million nano-bombs around your neck."

"That's for Arnie to verify." I nod toward the door. "We've have to get this to Ryan."

Shocked, Mary grabs my wrist. "Mom...Dad? What are you talking about?"

"Granddad James was... my father and Ondine *aren't* who they claim to be. The fact that they are Russian spies was always my cross to bear—until now. My father made amends for their treason by giving us this. It will end the terrorist act that created the embargoes." Jack kisses Mary's forehead. "Sorry honey, but we've got to get this to POTUS."

Mary sighs, but she knows the drill. She acknowledges it with strong hugs to Jack and me.

---

FOR ONCE, Ryan's anxiety about being summoned by Libby is for naught. She and Lee wait until the rest of our team connects by teleconference before declaring, "It turns out that James Craig's last living act was to hand over the passcodes that put an end to the flight and cellular embargoes. As of ten minutes ago, both crises have ended. In fifteen minutes, I will inform the American public that they can travel safely and use their cell devices."

Our team lets loose with whoops and hollers.

"Additionally, thanks to Black Tech's software, the malware that infected the White House's WPS has now been wiped clean," Libby adds. "I'll explain to the American public that the video they saw was a deepfake, how it was made, by whom, and why."

This time, we applaud our Commander-in-Chief.

"I will also make another announcement—about my new running mate."

Dominic texts the rest of our team: *What happened to Vice President Randall?*

Abu responds: *He wants to, quote-unquote, spend more time with his family.*

To which Emma adds: *In other words, Carol's team revealed him as the quote-unquote deep state operative who released the deepfakes.*

And Jack adds: *Finally! Correct use of the term "deep state," which is someone who misuses their role in a civil service or government-appointed position to undermine the rest of our selfless, hardworking governmental workforce.*

To which I text: *Well put, Mr. Craig.*

"...and I'm proud to announce that former President Lee Chiffray has graciously accepted my offer to be my Vice President," Libby announces.

I exclaim, "Wait... *WHAT?*"

Jack slaps his hand over my mouth.

I mumble a bit, but then I realize it's useless, so I give up.

And besides, I'm too tired to put up a fight. Not to mention I'm starving. Finally, Jack lets go. "Before I bite your hand off, let's head home and pick at what's left on the turkey," I suggest.

Jack kisses the tip of my nose. "You had me at 'home.'"

---

"I'M surprised at how much is left over!" My mouth is so full that even I can't even understand what I've just said.

"Me too," Jack admits. "That is if you said what I think you did. It was 'pass the gravy.' Am I right?"

Laughing, I shake my head. "No...but now that you mention it..."

As Jack hands me the gravy bowl, he adds, "Speaking about messy situations, I'll be honest: I was just as surprised as you about Libby's announcement regarding Lee as her running mate."

I almost choke on my mashed potatoes. "I know! Like, right? What the hell is he thinking?"

"My guess? Libby asked him to have her back, and he felt obligated to do it." To make his point, Jack pierces the air with his fork.

"Can't he do that in other ways?" I counter. "Heck, he could fund her campaign, and pull in other donors who are just as wealthy—and then be rewarded with a cabinet position, Say, as her Secretary of State."

"All that is true. But coming out of the tech sector, he knows best the lengths our foreign enemies will go to cause chaos stateside. And believe it or not, his public approval rating is higher than when he was in office. It's even higher than Libby's."

I sigh. "He seemed content with letting the foundation be his legacy."

"In this case, he feels it's the best way to show his duty to country," Jack replies. "To be honest, I'm impressed that he's stepped up."

"Here's hoping he doesn't regret it." I look over what's left of the turkey carcass. "Hey, get a load of this—no one took the wishbone!" I hold it out to him. "Want to put fate in the hands of a dead bird's clavicle?"

"I've bet on worse," Jack admits. "Go ahead, grab an end. Then count to three and we'll pull."

I hold it out to him. "Okay, here goes: one...two...*three!*"

He pulls—

And I do, too—

But I end up short. "Story of my life," I sigh.

"No, you are the story of *my* life." He holds up the winning part of the wishbone. "Since I first saw you, Donna Stone Craig, you've been my lucky charm."

I laugh. "That certainly sounds better than 'your turkey clavicle.'"

"I mean it." All humor is gone from Jack's voice. "How many times have you saved my life?"

"I...I really can't say."

"Exactly! And that's what a lucky charm does—protects

you and keeps the bad mojo away. And it brings good things into your life. There is nothing better than Mary, Jeff, and Trisha—not to mention Evan, who is another bonus if only to keep our family gender-balanced."

I giggle at that.

"Having met what's left of my family, you can better understand why I was drawn to yours."

My eyes get glassy. "I'm sorry that you had to handle Ondine that way."

"I'm not. My sister came to annihilate everything we'd built together: our family, our reputations, even our friendships..." His voice dies off. "But she didn't. She couldn't destroy us."

"No one will." I seal this promise with a kiss.

**THE END**

Other Books by Josie Brown

**The Extracurricular Series**

Books 1, 2, and 3

**The Totlandia Series**

The Onesies - Book 1 (Fall)

The Onesies - Book 2 (Winter)

The Onesies - Book 3 (Spring)

The Onesies - Book 4 (Summer)

The Twosies - Book 5 (Fall)

The Twosies – Book 6 (Winter)

The Twosies - Book 7 (Spring)

The Twosies - Book 8 (Summer)

**The True Hollywood Lies Series**

Hollywood Hunk

Hollywood Whore

**More Josie Brown Novels**

The Candidate

Secret Lives of Husbands and Wives

The Baby Planner

# How to Reach Josie


To write Josie, go to:
mailfromjosie@gmail.com

To find out more about Josie, or to get on her eLetter list for
book launch announcements, go to her website:
www.JosieBrown.com

You can also find her at:

www.AuthorProvocateur.com

twitter.com/JosieBrownCA

facebook.com/josiebrownauthor

pinterest.com/josiebrownca

instagram.com/josiebrownnovels

josiebrown.bsky.social